CW01658702

STORIES FROM ANCIENT IRAQ

Retold by Fran Hazelton
Introduction by Stephanie Dalley
Illustrations by Ed Coyne

The ENHEDUANNA Society

To Claire from Fran September 2015

The Enheduanna Society
P. O. Box 36855
Bloomsbury
London WC1N 1WB
www.zipang.org.uk

First published in 2006 by The Enheduanna Society
Second edition published in 2010

Text © Fran Hazelton
The moral right of Fran Hazelton to be identified as the author of this work has been asserted in accordance with the Copyright, Designs and Patents Act of 1988

Introduction © Dr Stephanie Dalley

All rights reserved. No part of this publication may be reproduced, stored in a retrieval system, or transmitted by any means, electronic, mechanical, photocopying, recording, or otherwise, without the prior written permission of both the copyright owner and the publisher.

British Library Cataloguing in Publication data
A catalogue record of this book is available from the British Library

ISBN 978-0-9554330-1-6

The cover illustration, by Sadiq Toma, is an artist's impresssion of the Sumerian woman portrayed in a statue now in the Louvre Museum, Paris.

Designed by Jane Walker
Edited by Ros Sales
Illustractions by Ed Coyne
Project Editor Viv Croot

Typeset by InterOffice Communications in Adobe Garamond Pro
Printed and bound in Great Britain

CONTENTS

DEDICATION

Dedicated to the memory of
DR JEREMY BLACK
founding patron of The Enheduanna Society

ACKNOWLEDGEMENTS

I became a Mesopotamian storyteller guided and supported by my fellow ZIPANG performers Fiona Collins, June Peters and Tara Jaff. My versions of these stories were written with the involvement of many people in the storytelling community, the Ancient Near East academic community and the Iraqi community in the United Kingdom. They listened to the retold stories, responded, advised, and encouraged. I am deeply grateful to all who helped.

The first edition of Stories from Ancient Iraq *was published in 2006 as a tribute to our shared cultural ancestores—the original storytellers of ancient Iraq. This edition will serve, I hope, not only as a tribute to the original Mesopotamian storytellers but also as a tool for those who take up the challenge of becoming modern Mespotamian storytellers.*

Fran Hazelton, London, 2010

THE LAND OF THE STORIES

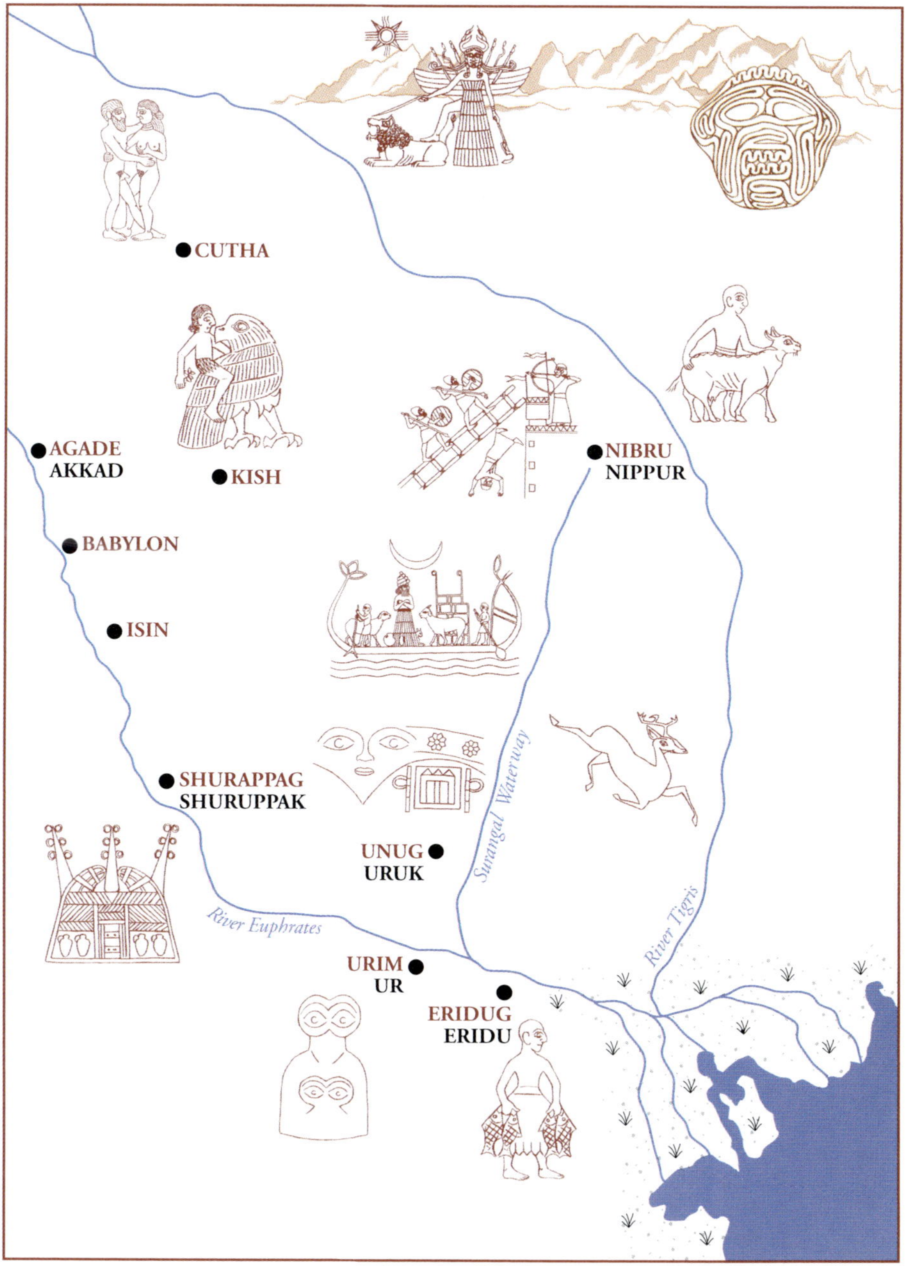

INTRODUCTION

ZIPANG, the storytelling group which Fran Hazelton set up and inspired, has mined a rich seam of new-old stories. Originally written some 4,000 years ago on the clay of Mesopotamia, they have come to light gradually through decades of scholarly activity. These retellings make good use of up-to-date scholarship, but are free from the pedantry and hesitations of academic translations. So they present wonderfully clear versions of very ancient tales.

The modern audience finds a surprising appeal despite the huge differences of era and culture. How can we account for this sympathy which crosses so many boundaries? Some answers lie in the fundamental questions about life and death which are explored through the metaphor of myth. The gods personify great natural forces, such as fertility and sterility, cunning intelligence and stupidity.

Even divine beings can make mistakes, acting in a short-sighted way that results in catastrophes; they can suffer anger and jealousy, or enjoy pleasure and laughter like mortals. What is the difference between mortals and immortals? How did their different spheres of influence arise? Why can mortals never become immortal, and why did human lifespan change after the Flood?

The gods built cities and dug channels for rivers, but no longer walk the earth, although they sometimes allow the destruction of their cities. They appointed mortal kings to rule on their behalf, but kings often behave badly, or fail to produce satisfactory heirs. Misuse of power can get out of control and threaten chaos.

Sumerian and Akkadian language speakers lived side-by-side for centuries in Mesopotamia, the one group having no known connection with other languages of the world, the other belonging to the Semitic group along with Arabic and Hebrew. Some stories told in Sumerian take up themes also known in Akkadian and vice versa, but others are confined to a single language tradition. Each ancient city had its own myths or versions of them and its own understanding of the pantheon, with local hero-gods and heroine-goddesses. This complexity of languages and cities helps to explain why the stories are so diverse.

With humour, paradox, and a pragmatic view of deeds both divine and mortal in which good and evil are intertwined, these Mesopotamian stories have the power to delight modern readers. ZIPANG is the skilful midwife of their renaissance.

Stephanie Dalley
Oriental Institute
Oxford, 2006

ADAPA

ADAPA

In southern Iraq, on the west bank of the River Euphrates, ten miles south of the ancient city of Ur, is a place named Abu Shahrein. To the west of Abu Shahrein is Iraq's great desert, with its rock-strewn wastelands and shifting sand dunes extending for hundreds of miles. At Abu Shahrein the fertile river plains of the Tigris and Euphrates come to an end. The marshes begin. The land becomes the sea. Abu Shahrein is the site of Eridu, the first city to appear in Sumer according to some of the ancient mythological texts written on clay tablets.

Eridu never became a great city like Uruk, Ur, Agade or Kish, but for thousands of years it was the cult centre for Ea, the god of fresh water and wisdom. When Iraqi archaeologists excavated Eridu in the 1940s they found the remains of a ziggurat temple built nearly 4,000 years ago. Under it were eighteen temples built one on top of the other. At the bottom was the original temple, built nearly 7,000 years ago. Eridu's reputation in the ancient mythology had been confirmed by modern archaeology.

This is an Eridu story originally written in Akkadian.

Long ago in Eridu there lived a wise man named Adapa. He was chosen by Ea, the god of fresh water and wisdom, to be the teacher of humanity. Ea gave Adapa eternal wisdom but not eternal life.

Adapa could answer many questions and do many things. Everyone admired and respected Adapa but he was humble. He helped the bakers bake bread, cooked, cleared the tables after meals and did the washing-up. Every day he caught fish for Ea's shrine. He could steer his boat without a rudder.

One day Adapa was sailing out to sea to catch fish when the hot, humid and heavy south wind suddenly blew up. It overturned Adapa's boat and tossed him into the water to visit the fish.

'May your wing be broken, south wind!' cried Adapa angrily.

No sooner were these words spoken than the wing of the south wind was broken. For seven days and seven nights there was no hot, humid and heavy south wind blowing over the land.

Up in heaven the sky-god, Anu, spoke to his messenger.

'There has been no hot, humid and heavy south wind blowing over the land for seven days and seven nights. Why not?'

'The wing of the south wind was broken,' said the messenger, 'by Adapa, the wise man of Eridu.'

'Bring Adapa to me!' said the sky-god Anu, getting up from his throne.

On earth the god of fresh water and wisdom, Ea, knew the ways of heaven.

He touched Adapa and spoke to him.

'Adapa, you must appear bereft and bedraggled. You will be

taken up to heaven to stand before the sky-god Anu. When you arrive at Anu's gate you will see two gods standing there, the shepherd-god Dumuzi and Gizzida, the Lord of the Good Tree. They will look at you and say: "Why are you bereft and bedraggled? For whom are you grieving?" You must say: "I am bereft and bedraggled because two gods have gone from the land. I am grieving for them." They will say: "Who are the two gods who have gone from the land?" You must say: "Dumuzi and Gizzida." The two gods will look at each other and laugh heartily. They will speak to the sky-god Anu on your behalf when you stand before him.

'You will be offered the bread of death. Don't eat it. You will be offered the water of death. Don't drink it. You will be offered oil. Smooth it into your skin. You will be offered a garment. Put it on. Do not ignore these instructions. Do as I say.'

The messenger from the sky-god Anu appeared.

'I have come for Adapa,' he said, 'the wise man of Eridu who broke the wing of the south wind.'

Adapa was taken along the road up to heaven. He arrived at the gate of the sky-god Anu. Two gods were standing there, the shepherd-god Dumuzi and Gizzida, the Lord of the Good Tree. They looked at Adapa.

'Why are you bereft and bedraggled?' they asked. 'For whom are you grieving?'

'I am bereft and bedraggled because two gods have gone from the land,' said Adapa. 'I am grieving for them.'

'Who are the two gods who have gone from the land?'

'Dumuzi and Gizzida.'

The two gods looked at each other and laughed heartily. Adapa was taken to the sky-god Anu and stood before him. Anu was angry.

'Why did you break the wing of the south wind?'

'I was sailing out to sea to catch fish for Ea's shrine in Eridu when the south wind suddenly blew up. It overturned my boat and tossed me into the water to visit the fish. "May your wing be broken, south wind," I cried angrily. No sooner were these words spoken than the wing of the south wind was broken. For seven days and seven nights there was no hot, humid and heavy south wind blowing over the land.'

Anu was still angry but the laughing gods Dumuzi and Gizzida spoke to him on Adapa's behalf and he calmed down.

'Poor Adapa is a mortal,' he said, 'but Ea taught him the ways of heaven so now he is troubled. Offer him the bread of eternal life. Offer him the water of eternal life. Offer him oil. Offer him a garment.'

They offered Adapa the bread of eternal life. He refused it. They offered him the water of eternal life. He refused it. They offered him oil. He smoothed it into his skin. They offered him a garment. He put it on.

The sky-god Anu looked at Adapa and laughed heartily.

'Adapa,' he said, 'Why did you refuse to eat the bread of eternal life? Why did you refuse to drink the water of eternal life? Don't you want to live forever?'

'Lord Ea told me not to eat and drink in heaven.'

Anu laughed.

'Ea has thwarted my plan,' he said. 'Now you, poor mortal, must return to earth. You will die but you will not be forgotten.'

So it was.

Adapa, the wise man of Eridu, looked up from the horizon to the heavens. He was overwhelmed. It was awesome.

Ea, the god of fresh water and wisdom, gave Adapa eternal wisdom, but not eternal life.

The sky-god Anu made him famous forever.

Praise be to the sky-god Anu.
Praise be to the god of fresh water and wisdom, Ea.
Praise be to Adapa, the wise man of Eridu.

THE GREAT FLOOD

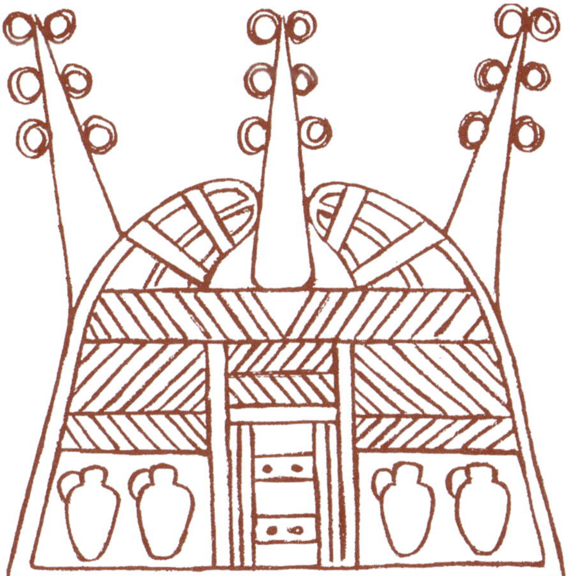

THE GREAT FLOOD

The story of the great flood was one of the most popular in ancient times. It was written in several languages and reworked to suit different regions and cultures. Here it is retold from the versions that have survived from ancient Iraq, written in both Sumerian and Akkadian. The Atrahasis flood story includes the creation of people and was recorded by the scribe Nur-Aya. The flood story retold by the character Ut-napishtim in The Epic of Gilgamesh *was recorded by the scribe Sin-liqe-unninni.*

In the beginning three of the great gods decided which of them would do what and where they would live. The sky-god, Anu, was the father of the gods. He had the greatest power and lived in the uppermost heaven. The almighty god, Ellil, was the leader of the gods and the terrifying force that subdued the land of Sumer. He lived on the earth. Ea was the god of fresh water and wisdom. He lived in the abzu, the place whence flow the waters of the earth and the wisdoms of the world.

Anu, Ellil, Ea and all the great gods were served by the lesser gods. They grew the food and brewed the beer. To water the land they opened the Tigris and Euphrates rivers, dug irrigation canals and kept them clear of clay and silt. They worked hard all day long, day after day for nearly four thousand years. They moaned. They groaned. They mumbled. They grumbled. One day they stopped working and cried out.

'Enough! Let us go to the house of Ellil and tell him he must free us from our work. It is too hard. We are ready to kill him!'

The lesser gods made a blazing bonfire of their spades and set off for the house of Ellil. When they got there it was the middle of the night. Ellil was asleep. Kalkal the gate-keeper bolted the gate. He woke up Nusku the chamberlain. Nusku woke up his master, Ellil.

'What is that noise?' asked Ellil.

'The lesser gods have surrounded your house. They raise their voices against you!'

'Make ready your weapon, Nusku. Stand by me.'

Nusku made ready his weapon. He stood by Ellil.

'Master,' he said, 'your face is as pale as a tamarisk flower. Are you afraid of the lesser gods? Send for Anu. Send for Ea. Summon an assembly of all the great gods.'

The sky-god Anu came down from the uppermost heaven. Ea came up from the abzu. All the great gods assembled in the house of Ellil.

Ellil spoke.

'The lesser gods have surrounded my house. They raise their voices against me. What is to be done?'

Anu spoke.

'Send Nusku to find out who is their leader.'

Nusku went to the lesser gods.

'I have come from the assembly of the great gods. Who is your leader?'

'We have no leader. We are all in this together. We have come to tell Ellil he must free us from our work. It is too hard. We are ready to kill him.'

When Ellil heard this he wept. He turned to Anu.

'I will show the lesser gods the power of Anu. One of them must be killed.'

'Their work is very hard,' said Anu. 'We have heard them moaning and groaning, mumbling and grumbling for nearly four thousand years.'

Ea spoke.

'Let us ask the mother of the gods, Mami, to make something to do the work of the lesser gods.'

'Yes!' said the gods.

Mami spoke.

'If Ea gives me purified wet clay I will make people to do the work of the lesser gods.'

'Yes!' said the gods.

Ea spoke.

'On the first day, the seventh day and the fifteenth day of the month there will be a purification. One of the lesser gods will be killed and mixed into wet clay so it has a mind and a beating heart forever. The killed god will never be forgotten.'

'Yes,' said the gods. 'So be it!'

And so it was. On the first day, the seventh day and fifteenth day of the month there was a purification. One of the lesser gods was killed and mixed into wet clay so it had a mind and a beating heart forever. The killed god would never be forgotten. Ea gave the clay to Mami. She passed it around the assembly of the gods. One by one they spat on it.

'Now,' said Mami, 'the people I make will have a voice. They will do the work of the lesser gods!'

'Yes!' said the gods.

They rushed forward to kiss Mami's feet.

'We used to call you "the mother of the gods". From now on we will call you "the queen of the gods!"'

Mami and Ea took the wet clay which had a mind, a beating heart and a voice into the chamber of destiny. Sitting there were fourteen womb-goddesses. Ea pummelled the pulsating clay. Mami sang her song. She pinched off fourteen pieces of clay. She put seven to her right and seven to her left. The domed birthing bricks were put in place. The fourteen womb-goddesses brought forth seven baby girls and seven baby boys.

The babies grew. The girls developed breasts. Hair appeared on the faces of the boys. Walking in the city squares and gardens the boys and girls chose each other and married. The couples joyfully cried 'Ishara!' and the goddess Ishtar rejoiced.

The wife created her home. The husband went out from the home with a spade. He dug irrigation canals and kept them clear of clay and silt to water the land, grow the food and brew the beer for the gods. After nine months the midwife put on her headscarf and belt. She opened the womb of the pregnant woman. The baby was born. The mother cut the umbilical cord.

So the people multiplied for nearly a thousand years. They raised their voices. The noise of their raised voices annoyed the almighty god Ellil. He summoned an assembly of the gods.

'The people you made,' he told them, 'have multiplied and raise their voices. The noise of their raised voices annoys me and I cannot sleep, so I will kill them all with diseases.'

Ellil sent the god of fate, Namtar, to kill all the people with diseases.

Beside the River Euphrates in the ancient city of Shuruppak lived a wise man named Atrahasis who had a mind, a beating heart and a voice. He prayed to the god of fresh water and wisdom.

'Ea,' he said. 'The people are being killed with diseases. What is to be done?'

He heard the voice of Ea.

'Tell the people to worship only the god of fate Namtar. They must build him a new temple and serve up offerings to him. Namtar will be touched and take away his hand. The diseases will disappear.'

Atrahasis spoke to the people. They began to worship only the god of fate Namtar. They built him a new temple and served up offerings to him. Namtar was touched and took away his hand. The diseases disappeared.

The people multiplied for nearly a thousand years. They raised their voices. The noise of their raised voices annoyed the almighty god Ellil. He summoned an assembly of the gods.

'The people you made,' he told them, 'have multiplied and raise their voices. The noise of their raised voices annoys me and I cannot sleep. I sent the god of fate Namtar to kill them all with diseases but some survived. Now I will send the storm-god, Adad, to kill them all with a drought.'

Ellil sent the storm-god Adad to kill all the people with a drought. Adad kept his rain inside the clouds and took the clouds away from the sky. The dark earth became white. Barley and vegetables died. People's faces were hollow with hunger and covered with scabs. The daughter closed her door to her mother. Parents ate their children to survive.

Beside the River Euphrates in the ancient city of Shuruppak lived a wise man named Atrahasis who had a mind, a beating heart and a voice. He prayed to the god of fresh water and wisdom, Ea.

'Ea,' he said. 'The people are being killed with a drought. What is to be done?'

Atrahasis heard no voice. He took his bed to the river's edge. He lay down to sleep and to dream. In his dream he heard the voice of Ea.

'Tell the people to worship only the storm-god Adad. They must build him a new temple and serve up offerings to him. Adad will be touched and take away his hand. The drought will disappear.'

Atrahasis spoke to the people. They began to worship only the storm-god Adad. They built him a new temple and served up offerings to him. Adad was touched and took away his hand. The drought disappeared.

The people multiplied for nearly a thousand years. They raised their voices. The noise of their raised voices annoyed the almighty god Ellil. He summoned an assembly of the gods. He was furious.

'The people you made,' he told the gods, 'have multiplied and raise their voices. The noise of their raised voices annoys me and I cannot sleep. I sent the god of fate Namtar to kill them all with diseases but some survived. I sent the storm-god Adad to kill them all with a drought but some survived. The secrets of the gods are being betrayed! Now I will send a great flood to kill all the people. None will survive!'

Ea bit his lip. Mami said nothing.

Beside the River Euphrates in the ancient city of Shuruppak lived a wise man named Atrahasis who had a mind, a beating heart and a voice. His house was built of reeds. Ea whispered into the reed wall of Atrahasis's house.

'Reed wall, reed wall, hear what I say. This house must be abandoned. A strong, square boat must be built. It must be covered with a roof so no rays of the sun come in. The boat must be filled with animals, birds, fish and the seeds of all things. It will be rained upon for six days and seven nights.'

Atrahasis heard the voice of Ea.

'What shall I tell the people?'

'Tell them that Ellil, the almighty god, and Ea, the god of fresh water and wisdom, disagree. Because you pray to Ea you must leave the realm of Ellil. You must go to the abzu, the place whence flow the waters of the earth and the wisdoms of the world.'

Atrahasis spoke to the people. He abandoned his reed house and built a strong, square boat. He covered it with a roof so no rays of the sun came in. He gave the workmen beer and wine as if they were celebrating the New Year. They lowered the boat into the river.

Atrahasis filled the boat with animals, birds, fish and the seeds of all things. He went on board with his wife and children. They sat down to eat. He could not eat. He vomited. He could not sleep. He walked back and forth. When night came he closed the hatch in the roof of his boat.

At dawn a huge dark cloud appeared on the horizon. Inside the cloud the storm-god Adad growled. The winds howled like wild asses. They bellowed like an angry bull. Everything went black.

The blazing torches of Adad's marching henchmen lit up the sky. Adad attacked the land like a ferocious army. He broke it to bits like a smashed clay pot. The claws of the Anzu bird ripped open the clouds. Rain fell for six days and seven nights.

The gods were terrified. They fled to the sky-god Anu in the uppermost heaven and cowered there like dogs. Mami, the queen of the gods, screamed like a woman in childbirth. Sweet-voiced Mami was wailing.

'Oh! Oh! How can Ellil do this to the people I made? They fill the ocean like fish spawn. They clog the rivers like drowned dragonflies. I hear them cry and I blame myself because I said nothing in the assembly of the gods. When will my weeping cease? How can I live with this grief? My lips are parched. My throat is dry. I should be drinking beer but who will brew it? Who will serve it?'

Sweet-voiced Mami wailed and the other gods wailed with her. They bleated like sheep, wet-faced with sorrow.

On the seventh day the rain stopped.

Atrahasis looked out of his boat. There was water all around him that went on and on for as far as he could see. It was flat and full of people who had turned into wet clay. He opened the hatch in the roof of his boat and the rays of the sun came in.

Atrahasis sat down and wept. His face was wet with tears. He looked again at the water. Patches of land had appeared. His boat was stuck on top of Mount Nimush. There it stayed for six days and seven nights.

On the seventh day Atrahasis released a dove. It found no branch to perch upon and returned. He released a swallow. It found no branch to perch upon and returned. He released a raven. It did not return. It had found a branch to perch upon, nibbled a berry, lifted its tail and preened itself.

Atrahasis walked from the boat with his wife, children and animals. He breathed in the fresh air and set about making a thanksgiving feast. He laid out fourteen jars of burning incense. The scented smoke arose. The pungent aroma curled, swirled, whirled and drifted wispily up towards the heavens. The gods appeared, like a bright semicircle of great flies with glittering wings.

Mami spoke.

'From now on I will always wear a lapis lazuli necklace that sparkles as a reminder of this moment. Let us feed on the thanksgiving feast. Ellil will not feast with us because he sent the great flood to kill all the people.'

But Ellil saw the thanksgiving feast and flew to it in a fury.

'How did these people survive?' he cried. 'Ea betrayed the secrets of the gods!'

'No,' said Ea. 'Atrahasis discovered what to do in a dream. I whispered into a reed wall. From now on, Ellil, when the people multiply and the noise of their raised voices annoys you so you cannot sleep, you should send a lion, a wolf or even a war to kill some of them but never again a great flood to kill them all!'

'What does Mami say?' said Ellil.

Mami looked at Ea and spoke.

'From now on when the people multiply, some women will never become pregnant. Some women will have dead babies. Some women will die in childbirth. Some babies will be snatched from their mothers' laps by the evil goddess Lamashtu.'

So it was. And so it is.

Ellil took the hands of Atrahasis and his wife. He touched their heads and spoke.

'Because you survived the great flood and saved the animals, birds, fish and seeds of all things you will become like gods. You will live forever where the rivers flow into the sea.'

Atrahasis and his wife became like gods. They lived forever where the rivers flow into the sea. They live there still.

Praise be to the sky-god Anu.
Praise be to the almighty god Ellil.
Praise be to the god of fresh water and wisdom, Ea.
Praise be to Mami, the queen of the gods.
Praise be to Atrahasis, the wise man of Shuruppak, who had a mind, a beating heart and a voice.

INANA & SHU-KALE-TUDA

INANA & SHU-KALE-TUDA

This is a Sumerian story about a raven, a date palm, a young man and the goddess Inana.

The goddess Inana possesses every power of destiny. She is the source of wonder in her temple in her city of Unug. One day Inana put on her cloak, left her temple and set off into the mountains. At the bottom of the mountains she stood among wild bulls. At the top of the mountains she stood among wild stags. She looked down upon the land and judged good and evil.

Below the land is the abzu, the place whence flow the waters of the earth and the wisdoms of the world. There, in his city of Eridu, lives Inana's father Enki, the god of fresh water and wisdom. On this day Enki was giving instructions to a raven.

'Raven,' he said, 'take some of the black eyeliner worn by the singing priests in my city of Eridu, chew it up, mix it with the oil and water found in a lapis lazuli bowl at the back of my temple and bury it in a vegetable garden in a furrow dug for leeks.'

The raven did exactly as he was told. He took some of the black eyeliner worn by the singing priests in Enki's city of Eridu, chewed it up, mixed it with the oil and water found in a lapis lazuli bowl at the back of Enki's temple and buried it in a vegetable garden in a furrow dug for leeks.

In that furrow a strange plant appeared. It stuck up like a leek but was unlike anything anyone had ever seen before. The raven stepped on to the ball of a shadouf and began raising water into the vegetable garden. He bumped the ball down and up, down and up, down and up, working like a man. Such a thing had never been seen before.

The strange plant began to grow. It grew and grew and grew until it became a date palm. The raven hoisted himself up and up and up to the top of the date palm. There he put the bits of chewed-up black eyeliner still on his beak into the date palm heart. What a date palm that strange plant became! Its palm heart leaves were shiny and lush. Its dry leaves were suitable for weaving. Its stiff leaves served to sweep the palace floors. Its delicious dates were good enough to feed the gods in their temples.

The raven carried on raising water into the vegetable garden. He bumped the ball of the shadouf down and up, down and up, down and up, working like a man until, at Enki's command, he stopped, stepped off the shadouf and disappeared into the abzu.

The young man in this story was the son of Igi-sig-sig. His name was Shu-kale-tuda. It was his job to build a well in his vegetable garden and water the plants, but he dug up their roots and they died. A mighty storm arose and blew dust from the mountains into Shu-kale-tuda's eyes. He rubbed his eyes and got out some of the dust but could not get it all out. He looked to the highlands and saw gods where the sun rises. He looked to the lowlands and saw gods where the sun sets. Then he saw a solitary goddess who possessed every power of destiny. Yes, it was the goddess Inana.

When Inana had gone around the earth, gone around the heavens, gone as far as Elam and Shubir, gone around the intertwined horizons of the heavens, she was tired. She lay down to sleep in the roots of a Euphrates poplar tree. Its branches shaded Shu-kale-tuda's vegetable garden morning, noon and night. From the edge of his garden Shu-kale-tuda stared at the goddess. Covering her sacred genitalia were seven powers of destiny. Shu-kale-tuda crept over to the poplar tree. He took up the seven powers of destiny. He made love to the goddess as she slept. He kissed her and walked away.

At dawn as the sun-god Utu arose, so too did the goddess Inana. She gazed upon herself and saw what had happened. She considered how to respond to the violation of her sacred genitalia.

She filled the wells of the land with blood. The earth was soaked with blood. The harvest was heavy with blood. The man who went for firewood drank blood. The girl who went for water drank blood. Everyone drank blood and wondered how long would this go on!

'I will punish that man,' said Inana.

She searched high and low but could not find Shu-kale-tuda.

He had gone to his father, Igi-sig-sig, who told him to hide in the city with his brothers so Inana would not find him in the mountains.

For a second time the goddess Inana considered how to respond to the violation of her sacred genitalia. She rose on a cloud surrounded by her priests and worshippers. A rainstorm went before her, a dust storm followed her.

'I will punish that man,' she said.

She searched high and low but could not find Shu-kale-tuda, who was hiding in the city with his brothers.

For a third time Inana considered how to respond to the violation of her sacred genitalia. She raised her hand and blocked every road in the land.

'I will punish that man,' she said.

She searched high and low but could not find Shu-kale-tuda, who was hiding in the city.

'Who will right this wrong done to me? Surely my father must!' cried Inana.

She turned her steps towards the abzu, the place whence flow the waters of the earth and the wisdoms of the world. There, in the city of Eridu, she held out her hands to her father.

'I will not return to my temple,' she told him, 'until you give me that man from the abzu.'

'So be it,' said Enki, the god of fresh water and wisdom.

The goddess Inana left the abzu and arched over the sky as a rainbow. When she touched the earth the north wind blew, the south wind blew and a mighty storm arose. Shu-kale-tuda, alone and afraid, made himself as small as he could. He was blown into the mountains and there Inana found him.

'You pig! You donkey! You dog!'

'My lady, it was my job to build a well in my vegetable garden and water the plants, but I dug up their roots and they died. Then a mighty storm arose and blew dust from the mountains into my eyes. I rubbed my eyes and got out some of the dust but couldn't get it all out. I looked to the highlands and saw gods where the sun rises. I looked to the lowlands and saw gods where the sun sets. Then I saw you, a solitary goddess who possesses every power of destiny.

'When you had gone around the earth, gone around the heavens, gone as far as Elam and Shubir, gone around the intertwined horizons of the heavens, you were tired. You lay down to sleep in the roots of a Euphrates poplar tree. Its branches shade my vegetable garden morning, noon and night. From the edge of my garden I stood and stared at you. Covering your sacred genitalia were seven powers of destiny. I crept over to the poplar tree. I took up the seven powers of destiny. I made love to you while you slept. I kissed you and...'

'Now you will die,' said Inana, 'which I never will for I am a goddess and you, Shu-kale-tuda, are a mortal man. You will surely die but your name will not be forgotten. The story of Shu-kale-tuda will be told in a sweet song sung pleasingly by young singers in the palace. The dairyman will sing your song as he tumbles his churns. The shepherd-boy will sing your song as he grazes his flocks. The gardener will sing your song as he waters his plants.'

So it was. And so it is.

Praise be to the goddess Inana, queen of the heavens and the earth.
Praise be to the goddess Inana, who possesses every power of destiny.
Praise be to the goddess Inana.

ETANA

ETANA

The image of a man flying on the back of a large bird is well known from the Greek myth of Ganymede. It also exists in Mesopotamian mythology. Etana, the king of the city of Kish, flies to heaven on the back of an eagle to find the herb of birth.

A picture of Etana flying on the back of an eagle is the only contemporary illustration of a Mesopotamian myth that has survived. The story itself has survived on fragments of clay tablets found at the sites of Susa, Assur and Nineveh. On those fragments the myth is written in Akkadian, but scholars believe it may have originated as a Sumerian story recorded by a scribe named Lu-Nanna. He lived about 4,000 years ago in the city of Ur.

One of the Sumerian king-lists states that Kish was the first city. The lists record that Etana, the king of Kish, was succeeded by his son, Balih. Behind this bald historical statement is the story of how that royal succession became possible. How Etana, the good king of Kish, flew to heaven on the back of an eagle to find the herb of birth.

The city of Kish was planned and built by the gods many, many years ago. At first there was no kingship. There was no throne, no lapis lazuli sceptre, no coned crown with a kingly headband. The goddess Ishtar searched high and low for a man to shepherd the people. She found Etana and he became the first king of Kish.

Beside the temple in the city of Kish, a poplar tree grew. In the branches of that poplar tree an eagle made his home. In the roots of the poplar tree a snake made his home. Soon there were baby snakes in the roots and baby eagles in the branches. The eagle spoke to the snake.

'Now we are both fathers, let us be friends and help each other feed our children.'

The snake was wary of the eagle.

'I will be your friend only if we make an agreement under the gaze of the sun-god, Shamash, touching the edge of his net that spreads over the earth.'

'Very well,' said the eagle.

The eagle and the snake made an agreement to be friends under the gaze of the sun-god Shamash and touching the edge of his net that spreads over the earth.

'Whoever breaks this agreement,' they said, 'may the mountain path be closed to him, may the flying arrow go straight to him, may he be caught in the net of the sun-god Shamash and punished.'

The snake and the eagle began to help each other feed their children. One day the eagle went hunting and came home with a donkey. The snake ate some of the donkey then turned away so the children could eat. The next day the snake went hunting and came home with a gazelle. The eagle ate some of the gazelle then turned away so the children could eat. The next day the eagle went hunting and came home with a lion. The snake ate some of the lion then turned away so the children could eat. The children of the eagle and the children of the snake became big and strong.

One day, when the snake was away hunting, wickedness entered the heart of the eagle.

'Now that my children are big and strong I will eat the children of the snake.'

'Don't do that!' said the eagle's wise young son. 'You made an agreement with the snake to be friends under the gaze of the sun-god Shamash and touching the edge of his net that spreads over the earth. If you break that agreement you will be caught in the net of Shamash and punished.'

The eagle ignored the words of his wise young son.

'I am not afraid. I will live high in the sky and fly down only to eat the tastiest morsels.'

The eagle flew down from the branches of the poplar tree. He entered the home of the snake, caught the snake's children and ate them. Then he flew away to live high in the sky.

When the snake came home from hunting he saw the black cloud left behind by the eagle. He saw the scratches in the earth gouged by the eagle's claws. He entered his home. It was empty. 'The eagle has eaten my children!'

The snake lay down and sobbed.

'Oh Shamash, the eagle has eaten my children. He broke the agreement we made to be friends under your gaze and touching the edge of your net that spreads over the earth. He must be caught and punished!'

The sun-god Shamash heard the snake's prayer and spoke to him.

'The eagle will be caught and punished. You will give him the punishment. Leave the city of Kish and go along the mountain path. There you will find a wild bull I have killed for you. Go inside the belly of the bull, make yourself at home and wait for the eagle. He will see the bull, fly down from the sky to eat the tastiest morsels, and go inside the belly of the bull. Catch the eagle, break both his wings, break both his legs, pull out his tail and all his feathers, throw him to the bottom of a very deep pit and leave him there to die of hunger and thirst.'

The snake left the city of Kish and went along the mountain path. He found the body of a dead wild bull with birds feeding on it. The snake went inside the belly of the bull, made himself at home, and waited for the eagle.

The eagle was flying high in the sky with his sons. He looked down and saw the bull with birds feeding on it.

'I will fly down and eat the tastiest morsels.'

'Don't do that,' said his wise young son. 'The snake may be waiting for you.'

The eagle ignored the words of his wise young son.

'I am not afraid.'

He flew down and landed on the back of the dead wild bull. The feeding birds flew away. The eagle stood on the back of the bull. He looked behind him then ate some of the bull. He looked in front of him then ate some of bull. He wanted to eat the tastiest morsels. He went inside the belly of the bull. The snake was waiting. He caught the eagle.

'You ate my children. Now you are caught. You will be punished. I will give you the punishment.'

'If you don't, I will reward you,' said the eagle.

'If I don't, I will have to take the punishment myself.'

The snake broke both the eagle's wings. He broke both the eagle's legs. He pulled out the eagle's tail and all his feathers. He threw the eagle to the bottom of a very deep pit, left him there to die of hunger and thirst, and slid away.

Alone at the bottom of a very deep pit, dying of hunger and thirst, with two broken wings, two broken legs, no tail and no feathers, the eagle prayed to the sun-god Shamash.

'Oh Shamash, what is the point of this punishment? Nobody can see me here. If you save my life I will praise you forever.'

The sun-god Shamash heard the eagle's prayer and spoke to him.

'You broke the agreement you made under my gaze and touching the edge of my net that spreads over the earth. You have been caught and punished. I cannot help you. But I will send a man who will, if you help him.'

The sun-god Shamash turned his gaze from the mountain path to the city of Kish, where good King Etana was praying.

'Oh Shamash, I have done no wrong. I have served up proper offerings to the gods. I have burned much incense with dream interpreters. I have been a good king. But I have no son to inherit my kingdom. I need the herb of birth. Please help me find it.'

The sun-god Shamash heard King Etana's prayer and spoke to him.

'Leave the city of Kish, go along the mountain path. There you will find a very deep pit. At the bottom of the pit is an eagle with two broken wings, two broken legs, no tail and no feathers. If you help him he will help you to find the herb of birth.'

King Etana left the city of Kish and went along the mountain path. He found the very deep pit. At the bottom of the pit was the eagle with two broken wings, two broken legs, no tail and no feathers.

'Will you help me find the herb of birth?' asked King Etana.

'If you help me out of this very deep pit,' replied the eagle.

The king helped the eagle out of the pit. For nine months he fed him and nursed him. The broken wings healed. The broken legs healed. The tail and feathers grew anew. The eagle was reborn.

'Now I will help you,' said the eagle to the king. 'I will fly around the mountains to find the herb of birth.'

The eagle flew around the mountains to find the herb of birth. He could not find it. He flew back to the king without it.

'I must take you to the goddess Ishtar. She is the keeper of the herb of birth. Sit on my back and clutch my feathers tightly.'

King Etana sat on the eagle's back and clutched his feathers tightly. The eagle flew high into the sky.

'Look down,' he said.

The king looked down.

'I see the city. The people are like ants. The rivers are like little streams.'

The eagle flew higher into the sky.

'Look down,' he said.

The king looked down.

'I see the land. It is like a garden. The sea is like a pond.'

The eagle flew higher into the sky.

'Look down,' he said.

The king looked down.

'I see nothing! Take me back to my city!'

The eagle tilted his body. The king fell off and tumbled towards the earth. The eagle swooped and caught the king on the tip of his wing. The eagle tilted his body. The king fell off and tumbled towards the earth. The eagle swooped and caught the king on the tip of his wing. The eagle tilted his body. The king fell off and tumbled towards the earth. The eagle swooped and caught the king on the tip of his wing just before he would have hit the ground with a thud. They were back in the city of Kish.

That night the king had a dream. The next day he told his friend the eagle.

'I dreamed the people of Kish were crying because I have no son to inherit my kingdom. My wife dreamed she was at my funeral and my ghost was there because I have no son to mourn me. Then I dreamed I flew with you to the gate of heaven. We bowed our heads and entered the realm of the gods. I saw a house with an open window. Inside was a beautiful woman. I flew in through the window. The beautiful woman was sitting on a throne. Beneath the throne was a growling lion. I went towards the throne. The lion leapt at me, roaring. I woke up terrified.'

The eagle smiled.

'I will take you to the goddess Ishtar. She is the keeper of the herb of birth. Sit on my back and hold my feathers tightly.'

King Etana sat on the back of the eagle and held his feathers tightly. The eagle flew high into the sky.

'Look down,' he said.

The king looked down.

'I see the city. The people are like ants. The rivers are like little streams.'

The eagle flew higher into the sky.

'Look down,' he said.

The king looked down.

'I see the land. It is like a garden. The sea is like a pond.'

The eagle flew higher into the sky.

The eagle and the king were at the gate of heaven. They bowed their heads and flew into the realm of the gods...

At this point the original writing comes to an end. A fragment from the bottom of the clay tablet has been lost, probably forever. But we know from the Sumerian king-lists that King Etana had a son named Balih who inherited his kingdom and became the king of Kish.

So praise be to the goddess Ishtar, who blessed King Etana with the herb of birth.
Praise be to the sun-god Shamash whose net spreads over the earth.

THE CURSING OF AGADE

THE CURSING OF AGADE

In the mythology of ancient Iraq kings were chosen by the goddess Inana. They also needed the approval of the almighty god, Enlil, who was 'the terrifying force that subdues the land of Sumer'. Enlil was worshipped in temples throughout Sumer but his home was his great temple, the Ekur, in the city of Nibru. For centuries this was the centre of Sumerian learning and religious authority. The idea that another temple in another city might try to rival it was unthinkable.

The scribal mythmakers of Nibru thought the unthinkable and wrote this Sumerian story as a terrifying cautionary tale. It describes what would happen to a city if its king defied the will of the almighty god Enlil and tried to build a temple to rival the Ekur. The city used as an example is Agade.

The fictional fate of Agade was the real fate of all the cities of ancient Iraq in the fullness of time. They rose and fell. Their glory days came and went. Then, over thousands of years, their magnificent buildings made of clay bricks crumbled into into dust.

One day the almighty god, Enlil, frowned on the cities of Unug and Kish. They fell like the bull of heaven slaughtered in the dust. Enlil gave power over the whole of Sumer to Sargon, the king of the city of Agade.

So it was that the goddess Inana went to live in the city of Agade. She was like a young man building a house for the first time or a young woman making her own home. She did not rest as she made sure the people of Agade had fine houses to live in and splendid food to eat. When they washed their hair and went out to festivals they had a great time. Friends dined with friends and foreign visitors flitted about like rare birds. They brought fantastic gifts from far away. Monkeys, lions, elephants, long-haired sheep, pedigree dogs and water buffalo jostled with the crowds in the streets and squares of Agade.

The goddess Inana filled the store-houses of Agade with barley. She filled its treasure-houses with gold, silver, copper, tin and lapis lazuli. She gave its old women the gift of wise counsel. She gave its old men the gift of eloquence. She gave its young men the gift of martial arts. She gave its young women the gift of entertaining. She gave its children the gift of merriment.

The nannies of the children who lived in the palace played musical instruments and the city resounded with the joyful sound of tigi drums. Outside the city there were zam-zams and flutes. The harbour was a happy place full of cargo ships. The foreign lands were peaceful, their people content.

The day dawned when the city of Agade had a new king, the grandson of Sargon, King Naram-Suen. With King Naram-Suen on the throne, the city walls of Agade rose to the heavens like a mountain. The goddess Inana opened the gates of the city. The goods of Sumer flowed in like the River Tigris flowing into the sea.

From the wilderness the Martu people brought wild cattle. From the blacklands the Meluhan people brought all sorts of exotic wares. The people of Elam and Shubir loaded themselves with produce as if they were pack-horses. The city gates were almost worn out with the influx of imports. The temple accountants easily fulfilled their monthly and New Year tax quotas. The goddess Inana received an overwhelming quantity of offerings. With all this prosperity, the goddess and the people longed for a new temple in the city of Agade.

But that was not the will of the almighty god Enlil, who lived in his temple, the Ekur, in the city of Nibru. Enlil's denial of the people's desire for a new temple sent a tremor of fear through the city. Even the goddess Inana was terrified. She abandoned the people of Agade like the lady of the house abandoning her handmaidens. She fled and took away the city's fighting spirit. Within five or ten days the other gods also abandoned Agade.

The greatness of Agade came to an end as if it were no more than the life of a tiny carp-fish swimming in deep waters. The other cities watched. Agade bowed its head like an elephant. They raised their horns like a wild bull. Agade dragged its head along the ground like a dying dragon. They looked down upon it disdainfully.

The king of Agade, King Naram-Suen, had a very bad dream. He dreamed the almighty god Enlil told him Agade would never again prosper. Its temples would be shattered. Its treasures would be scattered. The city was doomed. King Naram-Suen understood the meaning of the dream but told nobody. Instead, he went into mourning. He discarded his royal regalia, disabled his imperial chariot, covered up his ceremonial barge and sat with his head in his hands for seven years. Whoever saw a king sit with his head in his hands for seven years?

At the end of seven years, King Naram-Suen did some extispicy. He sent for a slaughtered kid-goat. He studied its entrails for a sign from the gods about building a new temple in the city of Agade. There was no sign. He sent for a second slaughtered kid-goat. He studied its entrails for a sign from the gods about building a new temple in the city of Agade. There was no sign. King Naram-Suen decided to act whatever the will of the almighty god Enlil.

The people of Agade were in disarray but King Naram-Suen mustered an army and marched through Sumer to the city of Nibru. There he entered the Ekur, the temple of the almighty god Enlil, like a wrestler entering the ring. Like a robber he placed tall ladders against the wall of the Ekur. He began to destroy it as if it were a mighty ship. He broke it like the rock in a gold or silver mine. He smashed it like a lapis lazuli mountain. He flattened it like a city flattened by the storm-god, Iskur.

Naram-Suen had great spades made that were suitable for digging up vast tracts of land with wide waters full of carp-fish. He used these spades to dig up the foundations of the Ekur. It was as if he was digging up the foundations of Sumer itself. He had great double-headed axes made with sharpened blades. These axes were suitable for chopping down whole forests of cedar trees. King Naram-Suen used them to attack the Ekur from above.

The Ekur, the temple of the almighty god Enlil in the city of Nibru, bowed its head to Naram-Suen, the king of the city of Agade. As it did so, the foreign lands bowed their heads to him. He took away the drainpipes of the Ekur. As he did so, the water of Sumer drained away. He took away the decorations of the Ekur. As he did so, the decorations of Sumer disappeared. He took away grain from the Ekur gate named Gate-from-which-grain-must-never-be-taken. As he did so, the grain of Sumer returned to the ground. He attacked the Peace Gate of the Ekur with a pickaxe. As he did so, the foreign lands rose up.

Now the soldiers of Agade saw inside the resting place of the almighty god Enlil. They saw the hidden treasure of the gods. The statues of gods on the pedestals of the Ekur are sacred, but King Naram-Suen threw them into a bonfire of trees uprooted from the temple garden. He bundled the gold, silver, copper, tin and lapis lazuli of the Ekur into sacks and took it to the Nibru harbour where his ships were waiting. When those ships set forth, loaded with the treasure of the Ekur, the city of Agade lost its mind completely.

Enlil, the almighty god Enlil, is the terrifying force that subdues the land of Sumer. When his temple, the Ekur, in the city of Nibru, was attacked and sacked by Naram-Suen, the king of the city of Agade, he was furious. He turned his gaze to the mountains and brought down the mountain people, the Gutians.

The Gutians have human intelligence but look like monkeys and behave like wild dogs. They swooped on to the plains of Sumer like a flock of small birds. They spread out like a net for catching animals. Nothing and nobody escaped them. They scattered the herds and herdsmen, took control of the rivers and roads, knocked the gates of the cities to the ground. Outside the cities—as in the days before cities existed—there was no grain in the fields, no fruit in the orchards, no fish in the fishponds. Some food was grown inside the city walls but it was scarce and prices soared. People starved. Those who died remained unburied.

In the heart of the city of Nibru there was an eerie silence. Wild dogs roamed in packs and devoured men even when they walked in twos and threes. Fierce fighting started. Noses were punched, teeth were knocked out, piles of severed heads appeared. The corpses of heroes were stacked high with the corpses of villains and traitors. The blood of the good mingled and flowed with the blood of the bad. From east to west, throughout the land of Sumer, the almighty god Enlil shrank his fine brick temples to small reed shrines and emptied the store-houses.

The people who survived this disaster gathered together as if at the end of the world. The young men sharpened their knives and cut themselves. The young women scratched their faces and tore out their hair. The chief lament-singer set up seven drums of lamentation. The people lamented to the almighty god Enlil as if they were his ancestors lamenting at his knees on the Sacred Mount. They pleaded with him not to forsake them.

'Oh my people! Oh my city!' they cried.

They lamented for seven days and seven nights. After seven days and seven nights of lamentation the almighty god Enlil returned to his resting place. He lay down in the ruins of the Ekur but could not sleep and would not eat. The other gods gathered around him and sprinkled cool water on to his blazing heart. They pleaded with him to punish the city of Agade.

'Let that city which destroyed the city of Nibru be destroyed itself. Completely.'

This was indeed the will of the almighty god Enlil.

All the gods turned on Agade and cursed it.

'Oh city of Agade, when you attacked the Ekur, the temple of the almighty god Enlil in the city of Nibru, it was as if you attacked Enlil himself. Now your walls will resound with wailing and crumble into dust. The statues of gods on your pedestals will tumble like drunken young men. Your clay will return to the abzu and be cursed. Your timber will return to the forest and be cursed. Your grain will return to the ground and be cursed.

'Your gold will be sold for the price of silver, your silver for the price of copper, your copper for the price of tin. Your harlot will hang herself in the brothel doorway. Your pregnant temple-woman will abort her unborn baby. Your cattle-slaughterer will slaughter his daughter. Your sheep-butcher will butcher his wife. Your strong working man will lose his strength. He will be unable to load pack-horses. He will sleep all day. Your people will starve.

'Those who once ate splendid food will now eat grass. The rich young man will chew the leather hinges on the front door of his father's house. The bird of misery, the ukuku bird, will nest in your doorways. The fox that frequents the ruins of long-dead cities will brush its tail along the fences of your sheepfolds where once sheep were fattened for festivals. The demons of the desert will howl all night and keep awake those who once were kept awake by the joyful sound of tigi drums.

'Your irrigation canals will fill with silt and clay. Their tow-paths will be overgrown with reeds. Lions and snakes will stop people walking along them. Your roads will be overgrown with weeds. Your river water will become undrinkable. Whoever thinks to rest in Agade will find no rest there. Whoever thinks to live in Agade will find no life there. The city of Agade will be destroyed. Completely.'

And so it was. That is what happened, in broad daylight, under the gaze of the sun-god, Utu.

The irrigation canals of Agade filled with silt and clay. Their towpaths were overgrown with reeds. Lions and snakes stopped people walking along them. The roads of Agade were overgrown with weeds. Its river water became undrinkable.

Whoever thought to rest in Agade found no rest there. Whoever thought to live in Agade found no life there. The city of Agade was destroyed. Completely.

Praise be to the goddess Inana, for the destruction of the city of Agade.

Praise be to the almighty god Enlil, who lives in his temple, the Ekur, in the city of Nibru, for he is the terrifying force that subdues the land of Sumer.

ERESHKIGAL & NERGAL

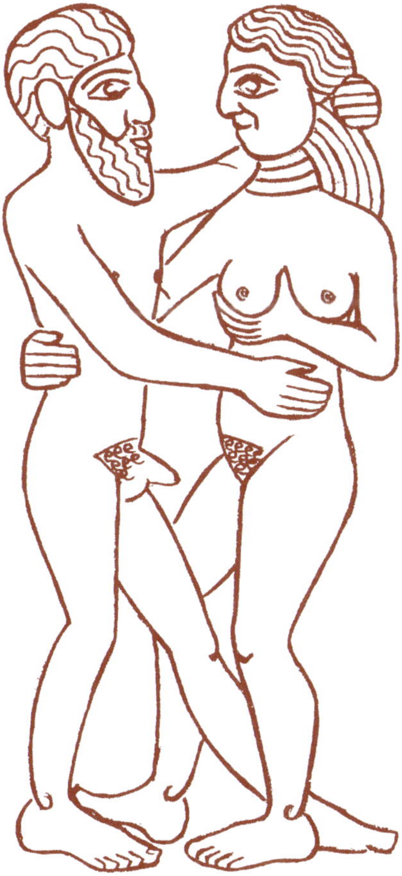

ERESHKIGAL & NERGAL

This is a love story originally written in Akkadian. The lovers are the goddess Ereshkigal, queen of the underworld, and Nergal, the god of death.

The gods in heaven were having a feast. Their host, the sky-god, Anu, spoke to his messenger.

'Take a message to my daughter Ereshkigal, the queen of the underworld. Tell her this. Because she cannot come up to the gods in heaven and we cannot go down to her in the underworld she must send a messenger to fetch her portion from the feast.'

The messenger of the sky-god Anu went down the long stairway of heaven. He came to the gate of the underworld.

'Open the gate.'

'May the gate bless you,' said the gate-keeper.

The gate-keeper took the messenger through the first gate of the underworld. He took him through the second gate, the third gate, the fourth gate, the fifth gate, the sixth gate. He took him through the seventh gate.

The messenger entered the throne-room of Ereshkigal. He knelt, kissed the floor in front of her and stood up very straight to deliver his message.

'The sky-god Anu has sent me to tell you this. Because you cannot go up to the gods in heaven and they cannot come down to you in the underworld, you must send a messenger to fetch your portion from the feast.'

'May peace be with the gods in heaven,' said Ereshkigal.

'Peace is with them. May peace be with you.'

The messenger of the sky-god Anu departed.

Ereshkigal spoke to her messenger, Namtar, the god of fate.

'Go up to heaven and fetch my portion from the feast of the gods.'

The god of fate Namtar went up the long stairway to heaven. He entered heaven's gate. The feasting gods fell silent. They all stepped aside and knelt to show him their respect. All, that is, except the god of death, Nergal. He showed no respect for the god of fate Namtar.

Namtar took Ereshkigal's portion from the feast of the gods. He returned to the underworld with tears in his eyes.

Ereshkigal spoke to him.

'That god who showed you no respect will come to me here in the underworld.'

Up in heaven that god, the god of death Nergal, was being spoken to by the god of fresh water and wisdom, Ea.

'Why did you show no respect for the god of fate Namtar? He is the messenger from Ereshkigal, the queen of the underworld. I gave you a nod and a wink but you ignored me.'

'I will go my own way.'

'When you go your own way, my son, you must be vigilant. In the underworld they will offer you a chair. Do not sit on it. They will offer you bread and meat. Do not eat it. They will offer you beer. Do not drink it. They will offer you a footbath. Do not wash your feet in it. Ereshkigal will bathe and put on a revealing gown. Do not be aroused. Do not do as men and women do.'

The god of death Nergal turned his face towards the underworld. He went the way of no return to the place of darkness where those who enter never leave but dwell forever without light, eating dust and clay, wearing feathers and crying like doves. He came to the gate of the underworld.

'Wait here,' said the gate-keeper. 'I will tell my lady there is a god at the gate.'

'A god at the gate?' said Ereshkigal.

She spoke to her messenger, the god of fate Namtar.

'See which god it is.'

When Namtar saw Nergal standing in the shadow of the gate of the underworld, his face went as pale as a tamarisk flower, his lips as black as tar.

'It is that god who showed me no respect,' he told Ereshkigal.

'Ah…' she said. 'No god should disrespect another or meddle in their realm. Can I eat and drink with the gods in heaven? No… Bring that god to me.'

The god of fate Namtar took the god of death Nergal through the first gate of the underworld. He took him through the second gate, the third gate, the fourth gate, the fifth gate, the sixth gate. He took him through the seventh gate.

Nergal entered the throne room of Ereshkigal. He knelt, kissed the floor in front of her and stood up very straight to deliver his message.

'The sky-god Anu has sent me here to sit in judgment.'

They offered him a chair. He did not sit on it. They offered him bread and meat. He did not eat it. They offered him beer. He did not drink it. They offered him a footbath. He did not wash his feet in it.

Ereshkigal bathed and put on a revealing gown. She let the god of death Nergal glimpse her body. At first he was not aroused. But then he could not resist his desire to do as men and women do. He embraced her. They lay together passionately for one day, two days, three days, four days, five days, six days.

On the seventh day Nergal whispered to Ereshigal.

'Let me go. I will return.'

Ereshkigal's lips darkened.

Nergal told the gate-keeper he must leave the underworld because he had a message from Ereshkigal for the sky-god Anu.

He went up the long stairway to heaven.

At heaven's gate he was greeted by the great gods—the sky-god Anu, the almighty god Ellil and the god of fresh water and wisdom, Ea.

'Nergal has returned!' they cried joyfully.

'Ereshkigal will want him back,' said Ea. 'He must be sprinkled with fresh water to keep him here in the land of the living. He must sit bare-headed among us, blinking and cringing.'

In the underworld Ereshkigal sprinkled fresh water around her throne-room as if she too were in the land of the living.

'That god sent by the sky-god Anu will eat and drink with us here in the underworld,' she said.

'My lady,' said Namtar, the god of fate, 'that god left before dawn. He has not come back.'

'Aaargh!'

Ereshkigal let out a cry of pain and fell from her throne to the floor. Her faced was soaked with tears when she arose.

'Nergal is my delight. I did not have enough of him before he left.'

'Send me up to heaven,' said Namtar. 'I will bring Nergal back to delight you.'

'Yes, go up to heaven,' said Ereshkigal. 'Tell the great gods this. I never knew the delights of girlhood. That god they sent delighted me. Now I cannot trust my judgment. If they do not send Nergal back to delight me I will raise the dead. They will outnumber the living and devour them.'

The god of fate Namtar went up the long stairway to heaven. At heaven's gate he was greeted by the great gods.

'Why are you here?'

'Ereshkigal has sent me to tell you this. She never knew the delights of girlhood. That god you sent has delighted her. Now she cannot trust her judgment. If you do not send Nergal back to delight her she will raise the dead. They will outnumber the living and devour them.'

'Come in. Look for your culprit. Take him.'

The god of fate Namtar looked for the god of death Nergal. He could not see him and went back to the underworld.

'I did not see Nergal in heaven,' he told Ereshkigal. 'But I saw a god who sat bared-headed among the gods, blinking and cringing.'

'That is Nergal!' said Ereshkigal, 'Ea has sprinkled him with fresh water to keep him in the land of the living. Bring me that god who sits bare-headed among the gods, blinking and cringing. Bring him here!'

The god of fate Namtar went up the long stairway to heaven. At heaven's gate he was greeted by the great gods.

'Why are you here?'

'Ereshkigal has sent me to bring her that god who sits bare-headed among you, blinking and cringing.'

'Come in. Look for your culprit. Take him.'

The god of fate Namtar looked for the god who sat bare-headed among the gods, blinking and cringing. He did not see him. Suddenly the god of death Nergal spoke.

'Let the god of fate Namtar be honoured!'

'Nergal, I have come for you,' said Namtar.

Namtar turned to return to the underworld.

'He will take me!' cried Nergal fearfully.

'Fear not,' said Ea, the god of fresh water and wisdom. 'I will give you seven demons.'

Nergal went down the long stairway of heaven. He came to the gate of the underworld. He ordered the seven demons to open all the seven gates.

'Watch out!' he shouted. 'I'm coming through!'

Nergal charged through the first gate, the second gate, the third gate, the fourth gate, the fifth gate, the sixth gate and the seventh gate. He burst into the throne-room of Ereshkigal. He thrust aside the god of fate Namtar. He ran up to Ereshkigal and laughed in her face. He grabbed her hair and dragged her from her throne to the floor. He was about to rip off her head.

'Don't kill me!' said Ereshkigal. 'Listen to me!'

Nergal relaxed his grip.

'I will be your wife. You can be my husband. I will put the powers of destiny into your hands. You will sit in judgment.'

Nergal was overwhelmed. He wept.

'Is this what you want from me? Then so be it!'

Nergal embraced Ereshkigal and wiped away her tears. They lay together passionately—Ereshkigal and Nergal—for one day, two days, three days, four days, five days, six days, seven days.

On the seventh day the sky-god Anu sent a message to his daughter.

'Ereshkigal, that god I sent you from the feast of the gods—the god of death Nergal—he is yours now, forever.'

Praise be to Ereshkigal, the queen of the underworld.
Praise be to Nergal, the god of death.

ENKI & NINMAH

ENKI & NINMAH

The face of a newborn baby wrinkled like a very old person is full of time. So it says in this Sumerian story. It tells how people were first made from clay by goddesses. Then the god of fresh water and wisdom, Enki, had a different idea. During a drunken quarrel with the goddess of the womb, Ninmah, he invented sexual intercourse.

At the beginning of time, when the heavens and earth came into being and destiny was determined, the mighty ocean mother of everything, Nammu, brought forth the great gods. They flew around with goddesses, who were everywhere, and the lesser gods came into being.

There were no people so the gods had to feed themselves. Seeds had to be planted, crops had to be watered, irrigation canals had to be cut and kept clear of silt and clay. Enki, the god of fresh water and wisdom, showed how this work should be done. The great gods supervised the work and the lesser gods did the work.

The lesser gods worked day in, day out, all day long, day after day. They were wretched. One day they stopped working.

'Enki is to blame for our wretchedness!' they cried.

Enki was asleep at home in the abzu, the place whence flow the waters of the earth and the wisdoms of the world. His mother Nammu woke him up.

'Enki! The lesser gods are wretched. They won't work to feed the gods. You must think of something else.'

Enki went to his thinking place, slapped his thigh and brought forth seven goddesses who could make people. He touched them one by one.

'Nammu,' he said, 'pummel the clay above the abzu. These seven goddesses will pick up the pummelled clay and from it make people. The goddess of the womb, Ninmah, will make the people work to feed the gods.'

And so it was. Nammu, the mighty ocean mother of everything, pummelled the clay above the abzu, the place whence flow the waters of the earth and the wisdoms of the world. The seven goddesses touched by Enki, the god of fresh water and wisdom, picked up the pummelled clay and from it made people. The goddess of the womb Ninmah made the people work to feed the gods.

The gods were delighted. They celebrated with a mighty feast. The goddesses ate delicious vegetables and salad. The sky-god, An, and the almighty god, Enlil, were served roasted kid-goat.

'Enki!' they declared. 'You are indeed a very great god. You alone determine destiny!'

Enki was drinking beer with Ninmah, the goddess of the womb, and now a quarrel began.

Ninmah spoke.

'It is how I make a person from clay that determines their destiny.'

Enki replied.

'However you make a person from clay, I will give them a life.'

Ninmah picked up some clay and made a man who could not close his outstretched hand.

'That man,' said Enki 'will be a royal courtier.'

Ninmah made a man with twisted feet who could not stand.

'That man,' said Enki, 'will be a silversmith.'

Ninmah made a woman who was blind.

'That woman,' said Enki, 'will be a leader of musicians.'

Ninmah made a man who could not keep his urine in. Enki sprinkled him with holy water and his disease disappeared.

Ninmah made a woman who could never have children.

'That woman,' said Enki, 'will be a weaver in the household of the queen.'

Ninmah made a man who could only think very slowly.

'That man,' said Enki, 'will be a servant in the palace.'

Ninmah made a person with no penis or vagina.

'That person,' said Enki, 'will be a Nibru eunuch and stand beside the king.'

Ninmah threw down the clay and was silent.

Enki spoke.

'Now I will make a person my way. A man will put his seed into a woman with his penis and a person will come forth from the wetness of her womb.'

And so it was. A man put his seed into a woman with his penis. After nine months the pregnant woman's waters broke. The domed birthing bricks were put in place. The woman pressed down and went into labour.

The sun set. The sun rose.

A little person came forth whose wrinkled face was full of time. Its head was wobbly. Its arms and legs were shaking. Its eyes did not work. Its spine did not work. Its bowels did not work.

Ninmah spoke to "Full-of-Time" but it did not reply. She offered it a bit of bread but it could not put its hand to its mouth.

'It's alive,' said Ninmah, 'but how will it live?'

'I gave a life to every person you made from clay,' said Enki. 'Now you must give a life to the person made my way.'

'Oh Enki!' cried Ninmah. 'What have you done? Making people was my realm and you were silent in it. Then you silenced me and took over. I lost my power when I was touched by you.'

'Indeed,' said Enki. 'One day "Full-of-Time" will climb down from your lap. "Full-of-Time" needs you to perfect my imperfections. Only then will "Full-of-Time" learn how to pray. Only then will "Full-of-Time" become the maker of my house. For the penis is a powerful thing, Ninmah. But a person has appeared through the wisdom and wonder of the womb which you, Ninmah, so graciously and gloriously provide. Let the gods be praised with hymns that sing of your heroic strength.'

With these fine words Ninmah could not disagree!

And so the quarrel ended.

Praise be to Ninmah, the goddess of the womb, for her heroic strength.
Praise be to our Lord Enki! How sweet it is to praise him!

GILGAMESH, ENKIDU & HUWAWA

GILGAMESH, ENKIDU & HUWAWA

The famous Epic of Gilgamesh *was recorded in Akkadian 3,000 years ago by a scribe named Sin-liqe-unninni. He drew on stories written in Sumerian 4,500 years ago. This is one of them.*

Long ago in the land of Sumer the day came when Gilgamesh, the king of Unug, decided to go to the cedar forest mountain and bring back precious cedar logs for splendid buildings in his city. He spoke to his servant, Enkidu.

'Enkidu, I will go to the cedar forest mountain and bring back precious cedar logs for splendid buildings in the city of Unug. No man is as tall as the mountains or as big as the land and no man can live beyond the end of his life. But I will make my name famous everywhere forever by going to the cedar forest mountain to bring back precious cedar logs for splendid buildings in my city and to praise the gods.'

'Master, the god who looks after the cedar forest mountain is the sun-god, Utu. Before you go there you should speak to him.'

Gilgamesh clasped a kid goat close to his chest as an offering. He raised his sword and prayed to the sun-god Utu.

'Utu, I will go to the cedar forest mountain. I need your help.'

The sun-god Utu spoke to Gilgamesh.

'Gilgamesh, why are you going to the cedar forest mountain? You have been chosen by the gods to be the king of the city of Unug.'

'In my city people die and there is sadness,' said Gilgamesh. 'When I look over the city wall I see dead bodies floating by in the river below. I know one day I too will be a dead body. No man is as tall as the mountains or as big as the land. No man can live beyond the end of his life. But I will make my name famous everywhere forever by going to the cedar forest mountain to bring back precious cedar logs for splendid buildings in my city and to praise the gods.'

The sun-god Utu heard Gilgamesh's prayer. He gave him seven blazing warrior stars to guide him to the cedar forest mountain. Gilgamesh was overjoyed. He ordered his herald to blow the horn and summon the men of Unug.

'Those of you with wives and children, go home,' he told them. 'I need fifty men without wives and children. Fifty brave young men like me who will follow me to the cedar forest mountain and bring back precious cedar logs for splendid buildings in the city of Unug.'

Fifty men without wives and children, fifty brave young men like Gilgamesh, followed him. They followed him to the bronze-smiths and armed themselves with daggers and axes. They followed him to the nearby woods and chopped down trees. They chopped down boxwood trees, walnut trees, juniper trees and willow trees, but not cedar trees. There were no cedar trees near the city of Unug. They followed Gilgamesh out of the city of Unug to find the cedar forest mountain, guided by seven blazing warrior stars.

They came to a mountain but found no cedar forest. They came to a second mountain and found no cedar forest. There was no cedar forest on the third mountain, the fourth mountain, the fifth mountain or the sixth mountain. When they came to the seventh mountain they found the cedar forest.

Gilgamesh, the king of the city of Unug, raised his axe and chopped down a mighty cedar tree. His servant Enkidu lopped off the branches. The men of Unug piled up precious cedar logs. Chop-chop-chop. Chop-chop-chop.

In the cedar forest mountain lived a terrifying creature named Huwawa. He guarded the cedar forest mountain for the gods with his seven auras of awesomeness. When Huwawa heard the chop-chop-chop of the axes his seven auras of awesomeness emitted vibrating rays, glimmering shimmers, shimmering glimmers. They made Gilgamesh, Enkidu and the men of Unug fall into a deep, deep sleep.

There was an eerie silence.

Enkidu was the first to wake up. He rubbed his eyes and shook

Gilgamesh but could not wake him. He whispered in Gilgamesh's ear.

'Gilgamesh, Gilgamesh, how long will you sleep? The mountains are disappearing as shadows creep across them and the sun-god Utu sinks into the bosom of his mother. Gilgamesh, Gilgamesh, how long will you sleep? Don't leave the men of Unug shivering in the mountains like puppies! Don't leave their widowed mothers spinning yarn in the courtyards of your city!'

Still Gilgamesh slept. Enkidu soaked a cloth in precious oil and rubbed it into Gilgamesh's chest. Gilgamesh woke up, sat up and bellowed at Enkidu.

'By the life of my mother and father!'

'Ssh!'

'Was I, Gilgamesh, the king of the city of Unug, asleep like a baby on my mother's lap? What made me fall into such a deep sleep? Was it mortal or divine? Until I find out I will not leave the cedar forest mountain. I will not go back to my city.'

'Master,' said Enkidu, 'it was Huwawa, the terrifying creature who lives in the cedar forest mountain and guards it for the gods with his seven auras of awesomeness. You have never seen Huwawa so you are not afraid of him. But I have and I am.

'Huwawa's chest is a roaring river in flood. His face is the face of a dragon with the mouth of a lion, a man-eating lion, with blood forever dripping from his teeth, his lips and his tongue. Huwawa is too strong for us, master.

'You may stay in the cedar forest mountain but I must go back to the city. When I tell your mother you are alive she will be delighted. If I then have to tell her you are dead she will weep.'

'We are strong enough if we stick together,' said Gilgamesh. 'Let's go on.'

'Let's go back,' said Enkidu. 'It will be terrible.'

'Let's go on,' said Gilgamesh. 'Let's look for Huwawa.'

'Huwawa's look is the look of death,' said Enkidu. 'If Huwawa shakes his head at you, you will never go back to your city.'

Suddenly Gilgamesh could not move. His toenails gripped the earth. He heard the voice of Huwawa.

'Oh Gilgamesh, What a brave young man you are! You tall strong sapling! You raging bull chosen by the gods to be the king of the city of Unug! You bearer of a sceptre with far-reaching power! Your mother surely knew how to give birth to a son! Your wet nurse surely knew how to breastfeed! Gilgamesh, touch the earth with both your hands under the gaze of the sun-god Utu.'

Gilgamesh touched the earth with both his hands under the gaze of the sun-god Utu. He spoke to Huwawa.

'Huwawa, do you want to be my kinsman? You can have my big sister as your wife. You can have my pretty little sister as your girlfriend. Just give up one of your auras and we'll be kinsmen.'

Huwawa gave up one of his auras. The men of Unug piled up precious cedar logs.

'Huwawa, do you want some cool water in a water-skin? Just give up one of your auras and we'll be kinsmen.'

Huwawa gave up another of his auras. The men of Unug piled up precious cedar logs.

'Huwawa, do you want some flour? It's the food of the gods. Just give up one of your auras and we'll be kinsmen.'

Huwawa gave up his third aura. The men of Unug piled up precious cedar logs.

'Huwawa, do you want some big shoes for your big feet? Just give up one of your auras and we'll be kinsmen.'

Huwawa gave up his fourth aura. The men of Unug piled up precious cedar logs.

'Huwawa, do you want some little shoes for your little feet? Just give up one of your auras and we'll be kinsmen.'

Huwawa gave up his fifth aura. The men of Unug piled up precious cedar logs.

'Huwawa, do you want some lapis lazuli? Just give up one of your auras and we'll be kinsmen.'

Huwawa gave up his sixth aura. The men of Unug piled up precious cedar logs.

'Huwawa, do you want some rock crystal found here in the mountains? Just give up one of your auras and we'll be kinsmen.'

Huwawa gave up his seventh aura. The men of Unug piled up precious cedar logs.

When Huwawa gave up his seventh aura Gilgamesh saw him standing there all alone. Gilgamesh stepped back as if to catch a snake. He leaned forward as if to kiss Huwawa. Instead, he punched him in the face. Huwawa scowled and showed his teeth.

'You are a false hero!'

'Sit down,' said Gilgamesh.

'Sit down,' said Enkidu.

Huwawa sat down and wept. Gilgamesh threw a rope over him as if he was a captured animal and tied his arms together at the elbows as a prisoner. Huwawa grabbed Gilgamesh's hand.

'Let me go,' he pleaded. 'I trusted you because you touched the earth with both your hands under the gaze of the sun-god Utu. Let me pray to the sun-god Utu who made me live here in the cedar forest mountain all alone guarding it for the gods with my seven auras of awesomeness.'

From the bottom of his kingly heart Gilgamesh pitied Huwawa.

'Let the trapped bird fly away,' he said. 'Let the prisoner run home to his mother. Let Huwawa become our porter and guide.'

'Master,' said Enkidu, 'what a brave young man you are! You tall strong sapling! You raging bull chosen by the gods to be the king of the city of Unug! You bearer of a sceptre with far-reaching power! Your mother surely knew how to give birth to a son. Your wet nurse surely knew how to breastfeed. 'One so mighty, master, who is so trusting, will surely be devoured by destiny and never know what happened. 'Let the trapped bird fly away? Let the prisoner run home to his mother? Let Huwawa become our porter and guide? We would never get back to our city!

'Is the captured soldier allowed to fight? No! Is the captured priestess allowed to use her holy room? No! Is the captured priest allowed to wear his wig? No!… No! No! No!'

Huwawa looked at Enkidu and spoke.

'How can you speak like that to Gilgamesh? He is the king of the city of Unug. You are his servant paid to run after him.'

This made Enkidu so furious that he took out his dagger and slashed Huwawa's throat. He raised his axe and chopped off Huwawa's head. Gilgamesh and Enkidu hastily stuffed Huwawa's head into a leather bag and took it on a raft along the river to the city of Nibru.

In Nibru they entered the Ekur, the temple of the almighty god, Enlil, who is the terrifying force that subdues the land of Sumer. They knelt down, kissed the ground and tipped Huwawa's head out of the leather bag as an offering. The almighty god Enlil looked at Huwawa's head and spoke.

'Gilgamesh, why did you do this? Did the gods decree that Huwawa should be slain and his name forgotten? You should have sat with Huwawa and shared your food and drink with him. You should have honoured Huwawa as the terrifying creature who lives in the cedar forest mountain and guards it for the gods with his seven auras of awesomeness.'

The almighty god Enlil gathered together the seven auras of awesomeness taken from Huwawa. The first aura he gave to the marshes. The second aura he gave to the mountains. The third aura he gave to the desert. The fourth aura he gave to the rivers. The fifth aura he gave to the lions. The sixth aura he gave to the palace. Huwawa's seventh aura of awesomeness the almighty god Enlil gave to the goddess of prisoners.

Praise be to Enlil, the almighty god Enlil, who is the terrifying force that subdues the land of Sumer.
Praise be to Gilgamesh, the king of the city of Unug.
Praise be to his servant, Enkidu.
Praise be to Nissaba, the goddess of storytelling.
And praise be to Huwawa, the terrifying creature who lived in the cedar forest mountain guarding it for the gods with his seven auras of awesomeness.

THE POOR CITIZEN OF NIPPUR

THE POOR CITIZEN OF NIPPUR

This Mesopotamian story was written on clay tablets in Akkadian 3,000 years ago. Ancient Iraq was a land of many cities. The best known of these is Babylon. But there was also Nippur, the city of learning, and Isin, the city of healing.

In the city of Nippur lived a man named Gimil-Ninurta. He was humble, poor and wretched. He had no gold, no silver, no bread, no beer, and only one shirt. But he had an idea.

'I'll take my shirt to the market and exchange it for a ram. I'll slaughter the ram, invite my family, friends and neighbours to a feast and my life will get better.'

He took his shirt to the market and came home not with a ram but with an old nanny-goat. He was about to slaughter the goat when he remembered he had no bread and no beer for a feast.

'My life will never get better,' said Gimil-Ninurta.

But he had another idea.

'I'll present myself to the mayor of Nippur, give him the goat and then my life will get better.'

He went with his goat to the mayor's house.

'Who are you?' said the gate-keeper.

'Gimil-Ninurta. A citizen of Nippur.'

'Wait here.'

'Who is it?' said the mayor.

'A citizen of Nippur.'

'A citizen of Nippur? Ha!'

'He has a goat.'

'He has a goat? Bring him in.' Gimil-Ninurta held his goat by the scruff of her neck with one hand and greeted the mayor with the other.

'You are most welcome,' said the mayor. 'Please be a guest at my feast.'

Gimil-Ninurta offered his goat to the mayor. The mayor took the goat and gave it to his servants.

'Slaughter the goat for a feast,' he said.

Then he whispered to the servants.

'At the feast give this citizen of Nippur a bone to eat with a little bit of gristle on it and a swig of third-rate beer. Then show him the door.'

And that is what happened. The mayor's servants slaughtered Gimil-Ninurta's goat for a feast. At the feast they gave Gimil-Ninurta a bone to eat with a little bit of gristle on it, and a swig of third-rate beer. Then they showed him the door. On his way out Gimil-Ninurta spoke to the gate-keeper.

'Your master tricked me. Now I'll trick him. Not once. Not twice. But three times. Tell him that from me.'

When the mayor heard what Gimil-Ninurta had said he laughed.

Gimil-Ninurta went from the mayor's house to the king's palace.

'Your majesty, please, let me have a bag of gold, a nobleman's shirt and a splendid chariot, just for one day.'

The king granted Gimil-Ninurta's wish.

Gimil-Ninurta put on the nobleman's shirt, picked up the bag of gold, stepped into the splendid chariot and drove around the city of Nippur.

With his bag of gold he bought a beautiful casket. He caught two birds, put them inside the casket and sealed the lid. Then he drove to the mayor's house.

When the mayor saw a nobleman in a splendid chariot driving towards his house he went out to greet him.

'My lord, you are most welcome. Please be a guest at my feast.'

'I have this casket with me,' said Gimil-Ninurta, looking very fine in his nobleman's shirt. 'It is full of the king's gold. The gold is the king's gift to the temple of Ellil, the almighty god of the city of Nippur. Will it be safe in your house?'

'Of course,' said the mayor. 'Please come in.'

This time Gimil-Ninurta was the mayor's guest with the beautiful casket in full view. He ate the best meat and drank the best beer. After the feast he talked to the mayor until the mayor fell asleep. Then he got up and broke the seal of the casket. The two birds inside the casket pushed open the lid and flew away with a mighty squawk. The mayor woke up.

'Look!' cried Gimil-Ninurta. 'The casket is empty! The king's gold has gone! What is to be done?'

He ripped his nobleman's shirt to shreds, grabbed the mayor, knocked him to the ground and beat him from head to toe until he was black and blue all over.

'Don't kill me!' cried the mayor. 'I'm a citizen of Nippur protected by the almighty god Ellil. You must not have my blood on your hands!'

'And you,' said Gimil-Ninurta, 'must replace the king's gift to the almighty god Enlil with double the amount of gold.'

'Of course,' said the mayor. 'And you, my lord, must accept my gift of not one but two new nobleman's shirts.'

'Of course,' said Gimil-Ninurta.

And that is what happened. On his way out Gimil-Ninurta spoke to the gate-keeper.

'Your master tricked me. Now I've tricked him. It's the first of three tricks. Tell him that from me.'

This time when the mayor heard what Gimil-Ninurta had said he was silent.

Gimil-Ninurta went from the mayor's house to the barber's shop. He had his head shaved in the style of a doctor from Isin, the city of healing, and picked up a clay pot full of water. Thus disguised he went to the mayor's house.

'Who are you?' said the gate-keeper.

'A doctor from Isin. I can heal wounds.

'Can you heal my wounds?' said the mayor.

'I can. But only in a room far from your servants.'

'Follow me.'

The mayor led Gimil-Ninurta to a room far from the servants. It had a hard earth floor and was lit only by a small fire.

'Lie on the floor,' said Gimil-Ninurta.

The mayor lay on the hard earth floor. Into the floor Gimil-Ninurta hammered five pegs. To the pegs he tied the mayor's two hands, two feet and neck. He picked up the clay pot, threw the water onto the fire, plunged the mayor into darkness and beat him from head to toe until he was black and blue all over.

'Ow! Ow! Ow!' cried the mayor. 'You certainly hit the spot! This healing hurts worse than my wounds!'

On his way out Gimil-Ninurta spoke to the gate-keeper.

'Your master tricked me. Now I've tricked him. It's the second of three tricks. Tell him that from me.'

This time when the mayor heard what Gimil-Ninurta had said he was nervous.

So was Gimil-Ninurta. He went from the mayor's house to the market. He looked around at the faces of the people until he found a man he could trust.

'Will you come with me to the mayor's house, gather a crowd, shout "I'm the man with the goat!" and run away?'

'Sure,' said his friend.

They went together to the mayor's house. Gimil-Ninurta hid under a nearby bridge. His ears were sticking up like the ears of an alert dog.

His friend gathered a crowd, shouted 'I'm the man with the goat!' and ran away. The mayor's servants charged out of the house and chased the man who was running away, leaving the mayor standing alone outside his door.

Gimil-Ninurta jumped from under the bridge, knocked the mayor to the ground and beat him from head to toe until he was black and blue all over.

'You tricked me. Now I've tricked you, not once, not twice but three times.'

Gimil-Ninurta, the poor citizen of Nippur, went for a walk in the meadows. The mayor of Nippur, now a humbler man, went for a walk in the city.

Praise be to Ellil, the almighty god of the city of Nippur!

THE MOON-GOD'S JOURNEY TO NIBRU

THE MOON-GOD'S JOURNEY TO NIBRU

This Sumerian story describes an invigorating journey by the moon-god, Nanna-Suen, in a magnificent ceremonial barge. He journeys from his city, Urim, to his parents' city, Nibru. His journey takes him past five cities where goddesses come out of their temples to offer him gifts. When he reaches the city of Nibru he unloads his gifts at the Ekur, the temple of his father, the almighty god Enlil. His father welcomes him and presents him with gifts to take back to Urim. They include the gift of long life in the palace.

The court storyteller concludes by praying that the king be invigorated for seven days and seven nights just as his kingdom has been invigorated by the moon-god's journey to Nibru.

The day came when the heroic moon-god, Nanna-Suen, son of the great mother-goddess, Ninlil, and the almighty god, Enlil, decided to go to his parents' city, Nibru.

'I will leave my city of Urim.' he said. 'I will go to my father and mother. I will go to Nibru. I will go to the shining city, the holy city, the great city, Nibru.

'Nibru is in a good place and its name is a good name. In Nibru black birch trees grow and white birch trees grow. Long before Dilmun existed date palms grew in Nibru and the great mother-goddess Ninlil wore fine linen.'

The moon-god Nanna-Suen began to build a magnificent barge. For its reeds he sent people to Tummal and Duashaga. For its tar he sent people to the abzu. For its planking, ribbing and beams he sent people to the Kugnuna forest, the Ebla forest, the cypress forest, the fragrant cedar forest in the mountains, and the juniper woodlands of Langi.

The reeds for the barge were brought from Tummal and Duashaga. The tar was brought from the abzu. The planking, ribbing and beams were brought from the Kugnuna forest, the Ebla forest, the cypress forest, the fragrant cedar forest in the mountains, and the juniper woodlands of Langi.

The sun-god, Utu, and the fire-god, Gibil, rejoiced with the moon-god Nanna-Suen.

Nanna-Suen spoke.

'I will go to the Ekur, the temple of the almighty god Enlil in the city of Nibru.'

For the Ekur, the moon-god Nanna-Suen will bring the bulls to the cow-pen, collect the fattened sheep and feed the goats. He will fill the water of the marshes with suhur carp-fish and eshtub carp-fish. He will make the reed-beds flourish. He will fill nests with the eggs of kuda birds, ubi birds and little azagun birds.

He will make six hundred ewes give birth to lambs by freeing the rams among them. He will make six hundred cows give birth to calves by freeing the bulls among them. He will make six hundred nanny-goats give birth to kid-goats by freeing the billy-goats among them. He will sprinkle those lambs, calves and kid-goats all along the banks of the Surungal Waterway.

The moon-god's magnificent barge left behind his city of Urim.

It set forth for the city of Ennegi. The goddess Ningirida brought from her temple what is kept in her temple.

'Welcome, oh barge! Barge of the moon-god!'

At her feet stood a bronze-covered gakkul-vat. With the tips of her fingers she removed its boxwood stopper.

'I will rub this stopper with precious oil. May syrup and wine abound for you. May many fishes frolic at the prow of your barge!'

The moon-god's magnificent barge did not unload.

'I will go to the city of Nibru,' said Nanna-Suen.

His magnificent barge left behind the city of Ennegi.

It set forth for the city of Larsam. The goddess Sherida brought from her temple what is kept in her temple.

'Welcome, oh barge! Barge of the moon-god!'

At her feet stood a bronze-covered gakkul-vat. With the tips of her fingers she removed its boxwood stopper.

'I will rub this stopper with precious oil. May syrup and wine abound for you. May many fishes frolic at the prow of your barge!'

The moon-god's magnificent barge did not unload.

'I will go to the city of Nibru,' said Nanna-Suen.

His magnificent barge left behind the city of Larsam.

It set forth for the city of Unug. The goddess Inana brought from her temple what is kept in her temple.

'Welcome, oh barge! Barge of the moon-god!'

At her feet stood a bronze-covered gakkul-vat. With the tips of her fingers she removed its boxwood stopper.

'I will rub this stopper with precious oil. May syrup and wine abound for you. May many fishes frolic at the prow of your barge!'

The moon-god's magnificent barge did not unload.

'I will go to the city of Nibru,' said Nanna-Suen.

His magnificent barge left behind the city of Unug.

It set forth for the city of Shuruppag. The goddess Nin-Unuga brought from her temple what is kept in her temple.

'Welcome, oh barge! Barge of the moon-god!'

At her feet stood a bronze-covered gakkul-vat. With the tips of her fingers she removed its boxwood stopper.

'I will rub this stopper with precious oil. May syrup and wine abound for you. May many fishes frolic at the prow of your barge!'

The moon-god's magnificent barge did not unload.

'I will go to the city of Nibru,' said Nanna-Suen.

His magnificent barge left behind the city of Shurappag.

It set forth for the city of Tummal. The goddess Ninlil brought from her temple what is kept in her temple.

'Welcome, oh barge! Barge of the moon-god, my son!'

At her feet stood a bronze-covered gakkul-vat. With the tips of her fingers she removed its boxwood stopper.

'I will rub this stopper with precious oil. May syrup and wine abound for you. May many fishes frolic at the prow of your barge!'

The moon-god's magnificent barge did not unload.

'I will go to the city of Nibru,' said Nanna-Suen.

His magnificent barge left behind the city of Tummal.

It set forth for the city of Nibru.

At Nibru's splendid harbour the moon-god Nanna-Suen docked his magnificent barge. He stepped up to his father's temple, the Ekur. He called out to his father's gate-keeper, Kalkal.

'Open up the temple, Kalkal! Open the temple gate! I bring gifts for the Ekur, the temple of the almighty god Enlil in the city of Nibru. I, the moon-god Nanna-Suen, have brought the bulls to the cow-pen, collected the fattened sheep and fed the goats. I have filled the water of the marshes with suhur carp-fish and eshtub carp-fish. I have made the reed-beds flourish and filled nests with the eggs of kuda birds, ubi birds and little azagun birds.

'I have made six hundred ewes give birth to lambs by freeing the rams among them. I have made six hundred cows give birth to calves by freeing the bulls among them. I have made six hundred nanny-goats give birth to kid-goats by freeing the billy-goats among them. I have sprinkled the lambs, calves and kid-goats all along the banks of the Surungal Waterway.

'Open the temple gate, Kalkal! I will unload all the gifts in my magnificent barge, from the first in its prow to the last in its stern!'

Kalkal the gate-keeper, the man in charge of the bolt-handle, opened the temple gate joyfully. The moon-god Nanna-Suen unloaded all the gifts in his magnificent barge, from the first in its prow to the last in its stern.

The almighty god Enlil was pleased by the gifts from his son.

'Bring my son the best bread from the temple. Pour him the best beer from the tall tilimda-vessel. Give sweet cakes to my little son, who loves to eat sweet cakes.'

The moon-god Nanna-Suen ate and drank.

He spoke to his father.

'Thank you for what you have given me to eat, father. Thank you for what you have given me to drink. Wherever you raise your eyes there is kingship. Wherever you raise your eyes there is abundance. Give to me now, father, for I will return to Urim.

'In the river give me carp-fish floods, for I will return to Urim. In the marshes give me kuda birds, for I will return to Urim. In the fields give me speckled barley, for I will return to Urim. In the forest give me fallow deer, for I will return to Urim. In the desert give me mashgurum trees, for I will return to Urim. In the orchards give me syrup and wine, for I will return to Urim. In the palace give me long life, for I will return to Urim.'

The almighty god Enlil gave to the moon-god Nanna-Suen. The moon-god returned to Urim.

In the river Enlil gave carp-fish floods. The moon-god returned to Urim. In the marshes Enlil gave kuda birds. The moon-god returned to Urim. In the fields Enlil gave speckled barley. The moon-god returned to Urim. In the forest Enlil gave fallow deer. The moon-god returned to Urim. In the desert Enlil gave mashgurum trees. The moon-god returned to Urim. In the orchards Enlil gave syrup and wine. The moon-god returned to Urim. In the palace Enlil gave long life. The moon-god returned to Urim.

For the almighty god Enlil and for the great mother-goddess Ninlil—oh my king, seated upon your throne—may their son the moon-god, Nanna-Suen, invigorate you for seven days and seven nights, as his journey to Nibru has invigorated the land.

Praise be to the moon-god Nanna-Suen, the heroic moon-god, Nanna-Suen.

INANA & THE KING

INANA & THE KING

This Sumerian story comes from A Hymn to Inana for Iddin-Dagin.

Every day, when the sun goes down, Inana's star arises. Every month, when the moon goes dark, Inana's powers are perfected. Every year, when the spring begins, the king goes to bed with Inana and they make love. The land flourishes and the people prosper.

Long ago, in the land of Sumer, the light was fading as the day came to a close. The goddess Inana heroically arose as the evening star. Her brilliance lit up the heavens like a blazing torch.

People stopped to gaze at her. Oxen in harnesses lifted their heads. Sheep in sheepfolds kicked up the dust. Four-legged beasts of the plains and reed-beds, fishes that swam in deep waters, birds flying high in the sky all went home to their resting places.

Every living thing worshipped Inana. Throughout the land of Sumer food was prepared for her and young men found pleasure with their wives. Praise be to the goddess Inana, our lady of the evening.

Every night, in the darkness of night, Inana shone as brightly as the moon or the noon-day sun while the people slept. Their storehouses were full. They gave themselves up to her judgment. She restrained the wicked. She favoured the just. She determined destinies. Praise be to the goddess Inana, whose grandeur extends to the edges of the heavens.

Every day, at the break of day, Inana appeared as the morning star, smiling joyfully upon her people, whose personal gods were with them.

For Inana, they loaded tables with cheeses and dates, honey cakes and fruits, sunrise wine and early morning beer. For Inana, fattened sheep were slaughtered and roasted. For Inana, the aroma of incense rose as if from a forest of sweet-scented cedar trees. For Inana, the traveller found his way. For Inana, the cowherd sang his song. For Inana, temples were built and the land trembled.

Praise be to the goddess Inana who possesses every power of destiny, which she was given by her father, Enki, the god of fresh water and wisdom, when she visited him in the abzu, the place whence flow the waters of the earth and the wisdoms of the world.

Every month, at the turning of the moon, Inana's powers were perfected. She took her place in the heavens among the greatest of the gods. The lesser gods gathered around her and bowed. She listened to their supplications and determined the destiny of the land.

The people of Sumer, the black-haired people, paraded for Inana to the sound of drums played with sacred drum-sticks.

First came the glamour boys dressed in divine leather, their carefully combed hair adorned with ribbons. They paraded for Inana. Then came the wise old women, the wisest one among them accompanying the king. They paraded for Inana. Then came the drummers, playing drums with sacred drumsticks. They paraded for Inana. Then came the soldiers, swords and spears at the ready. They paraded for Inana. Then came those whose garments had both a feminine side and a masculine side. They paraded for Inana. Then came those who competed with twirling, swirling, whirling streamers of many colours. They paraded for Inana. Then came the captives in neck-stocks, singing their songs. They paraded for Inana. Then came the curly-haired girls from the temple. They paraded for Inana. Then came the priests who dipped their daggers in blood and splashed it from side to side. They paraded for Inana.

The sound of the drums became louder and louder until blood was poured on the temple platform. Praise be to the goddess Inana, who watches her flocks from the heavens.

Every year, at the beginning of spring, Inana's bed was prepared in the palace—the place that governed the land—and the people gathered there. Scented oils were laid around the bed. Scented grasses were laid around the bed. A beautiful cover of love was laid over the bed. The goddess Inana bathed her thighs for the thighs of the king. He, with his head held high, caressed her. Together, on the sacred bed, the goddess and the king rejoiced.

'You are my beloved,' said Inana.

The king commanded a mighty feast to honour Inana. The goddess bade him sit beside her to bask in her glow.

For the people of Sumer, the black-haired people, there was more to eat and drink than you could ever imagine. There was music loud enough to keep away the southern storms. There were songs to soothe and delight the hearts of the gods.

'Long live the king! Praise be to the goddess Inana!'

Every day, when the sun goes down, Inana's star arises. Every month, when the moon goes dark, Inana's powers are perfected. Every year, when the spring begins, the king goes to bed with Inana and they make love. The land flourishes and the people prosper.

> Praise be to the goddess Inana, the queen of the heavens and the earth, for she is the oldest daughter of the moon, and youth eternal.
>
> Praise be to the goddess Inana!

DUMUZID'S DREAM

DUMUZID'S DREAM

In the mythology of ancient Iraq the shepherd-god, Dumuzid, is the husband of the goddess Inana. Kings identified with him and ritually married Inana in the sacred marriage rite to ensure the fertility of the land.

In the story Inana's Descent to the Underworld *the goddess can only return to the land of the living by giving Dumuzid to underworld demons as a substitute for herself. As a god who every year dies and rises from the dead, Dumuzid represents annual decay and renewal.*

Inana's Descent to the Underworld *and* Dumuzid's Dream *also reflect a grim reality of life in ancient Iraq. Shepherds, farmers and other young men were often in danger of being seized by government press-gangs for forced labour or military service. Female lamentation for the loss of Dumuzid was an enduring feature of Mesopotamian culture.*

Dumuzid is mentioned in the Bible by Ezekiel using the Hebrew form of his name, 'Tammuz'. 'Tammuz' is still used in Iraqi Arabic as the name for the month of July, a calendar tradition that can be traced back at least 3,000 years.

The young shepherd-god, Dumuzid, was walking alone in the land. His heart was full of sorrow. It overflowed with tears and he wept.

'Mountains of the land, will you weep for me when I am dead? Marshes of the land, will you weep for me when I am dead? Frogs and crabs in the river, will you weep for me when I am dead? Will you tell my mother I am dead when she calls for me to bring bread to her, not knowing I am dead? Will you weep for me like my sister Geshtinana?'

The shepherd-god Dumuzid lay down to dream. He slept. He awoke. He rubbed his eyes. He was terrified.

'Geshtinana! My little sister who sings sweet songs, my wise scribe who writes on clay tablets, my clever girl who knows the meaning of dreams, come, let me tell you my dream.

'In my dream uprooted reeds sprouted around me, a single reed shook its head at me. A double reed split apart. Tall trees towered over me.

'The brazier in my sheepfold was full of water. Beside the brazier milk-churn covers lay discarded. My special cup was gone from its hook. My shepherd's crook was missing. A falcon snatched a lamb from inside the sheepfold, an owl snatched a sparrow from the sheepfold fence. My milk-churns lay on their sides with the milk spilt. All my cups were smashed to bits on the ground. Dumuzid was dead, his sheepfold deserted. The black beards of billy-goats swished in the dust. The sharp hooves of rams scratched the earth...'

'Stop, Dumuzid!' cried Geshtinana. 'I can hear no more of this terrible dream! The uprooted reeds sprouting around you are evil men coming to get you. The single reed shaking its head at you is our mother. The double reed split apart is you and I. The tall trees towering over you are the evil men overpowering you.

'The water in your brazier—this means your sheepfold will be destroyed. The discarded milk-churn covers—this means the evil men will do it. Your special cup gone from its hook—this means you will be taken from your mother who held you on her lap. Your missing shepherd's crook—this means the evil men will break it. The falcon snatching a lamb from inside the sheepfold, the owl snatching a sparrow from the sheepfold fence—this means the evil men will destroy the sheepfold inside and out. Your milk-churns on their sides with the milk spilt, your cups smashed to bits on the ground, Dumuzid dead and his sheepfold deserted—this means you will be captured and handcuffed with your arms twisted behind your back.

'The black beards of billy-goats swishing in the dust are tufts of black hair torn from my head and swirling in the wind. The sharp hooves of rams scratching the earth are my finger-nails like boxwood needles tearing the skin from my face, my belly, and my thighs...'

'Stop, Geshtinana!' cried Dumuzid. 'Geshtinana, with your hair torn from your head, with your skin torn from your face, your belly, and your thighs, you must go to the top of the hill and look out for the evil men. They will come in barges on the river. They will bring the handcuffs from which no man can escape.'

Geshtinana went to the top of the hill with her girl-friend, Geshtindudu. They looked out for the evil men.

‘I see them!’ said Geshtindudu. ‘The evil men are coming to get Dumuzid!”

Geshtinana ran to her brother.

‘Dumuzid, the evil men are coming. Hide in the grasses and keep your head down.’

‘I will hide in the grasses and keep my head down. Don’t tell them where I am. I will hide in the short grasses. Don’t tell them where I am. I will hide in the long grasses. Don’t tell them where I am. I will hide in the ditches of Arali. Don’t tell them where I am.’

‘If I tell the evil men where you are, may I be eaten alive by your big black dog. You must tell your friend what is happening,’ said Geshtinana.

Dumuzid told his friend.

‘The evil men are coming to get me. I will hide in the grasses and keep my head down. Don’t tell them where I am. I will hide in the short grasses. Don’t tell them where I am. I will hide in the long grasses. Don’t tell them where I am. I will hide in the ditches of Arali. Don’t tell them where I am.’

‘If I tell the evil men where you are may I be eaten alive by your big black dog,’ said Dumuzid’s friend.

The seven evil men who came to get Dumuzid were an inhuman gang. They never exchanged gifts, caressed their wives or kissed their children. They came from four different cities of Sumer. The two from Adab would sit at your table then report you to the palace. The two from Urim had skull-crushing clubs dangling from their belts.

'Let's go get Dumuzid!' they said.

In Dumuzid's sheepfold they found his sister Geshtinana.

'Where is Dumuzid?'

They offered her a river full of water. They offered her a field full of barley. She refused them.

'No sister betrays her brother,' said one of the evil men. 'Let's go find Dumuzid's friend.'

They found Dumuzid's friend. They offered him a river full of water. They offered him a field full of barley. He accepted them.

'Dumuzid is hiding in the grasses and keeping his head down,' he told the evil men. 'He is hiding in the short grasses but I don't know where.'

They looked for Dumuzid in the short grasses. They did not find him.

'Dumuzid is hiding in the long grasses but I don't know where.'

They looked for Dumuzid in the long grasses. They did not find him.

'Dumuzid is hiding in the ditches of Arali but I don't know where.'

They looked for Dumuzid in the ditches of Arali. They found him. Dumuzid turned pale and wept.

'My sister took care of my life. My friend took care of my death. If her child is lost in the city may someone take care of it. If his child is lost in the city may no-one take care of it.'

The evil men surrounded Dumuzid. They had a rope, a stick and a net. They handcuffed him with his arms twisted behind his back. Dumuzid looked up to the sun-god, Utu.

'Utu, I am the husband of your sister, the goddess Inana. I bring food to her temple, the E-ana. I bring wedding gifts to her city of Unug. I kiss her holy lips. I dance between her holy knees. Please, change my hands and feet into the hands and feet of a gazelle so that I can escape from these evil men and go to Ku-biresh-dildaresh.'

The sun-god Utu accepted Dumuzid's tears. Mercifully, he changed his hands and feet into the hands and feet of a gazelle. Dumuzid escaped from the evil men and went to Ku-biresh-dildaresh. The evil men looked for Dumuzid. They did not find him.

'We must go to Ku-biresh-dildaresh,' they said.

They went to Ku-biresh-dildaresh. They found Dumuzid and surrounded him. They had a rope, a stick and a net. For a second time the evil men captured Dumuzid and handcuffed him with his arms twisted behind his back. Again Dumuzid looked up to the sun-god Utu.

'Utu, I am the husband of your sister, the goddess Inana. I bring food to her temple, the E-ana. I bring wedding gifts to her city of

Unug. I kiss her holy lips. I dance between her holy knees. Please, change my hands and feet into the hands and feet of a gazelle so I can escape from these evil men and go to the house of the Old Woman Belili.'

Again the sun-god Utu accepted Dumuzid's tears. He mercifully changed his hands and feet into the hands and feet of a gazelle. For a second time Dumuzid escaped from the evil men. He went to the house of the Old Woman Belili.

'I am no ordinary man,' he told her. 'I am the husband of the goddess Inana. Please give me something to eat and drink.'

The Old Woman Belili gave Dumuzid something to eat and drink. She went outside her house. The evil men saw her.

'That old woman knows where Dumuzid is,' they said. 'We must go to her house.'

The evil men went to the house of the Old Woman Belili. They found Dumuzid and surrounded him. They had a rope, a stick and a net. For a third time they captured Dumuzid and handcuffed him with his arms twisted behind his back. Again Dumuzid looked up to the sun-god Utu.

'Utu, I am the husband of your sister, the goddess Inana. I bring food to her temple, the E-ana. I bring wedding gifts to her city of Unug. I kiss her holy lips. I dance between her holy knees. Please change my hands and feet into the hands and feet of a gazelle so I can escape from these evil men and go to the sheepfold.'

Again the sun-god Utu accepted Dumuzid's tears. He mercifully changed his hands and feet into the hands and feet of a gazelle. For a third time the shepherd-god Dumuzi escaped from the evil men. He went to the sheepfold.

When Dumuzid's sister Geshtinana saw him she cried out to heaven. Her cry covered the earth like a linen cloth. She tore out her hair in black tufts. She tore the skin from her face, her belly, and her thighs, outwardly and inwardly.

'Dumuzid is in the sheepfold,' said the evil men.

The first evil man entered the sheepfold with a mighty shout. The second evil man poured water on the brazier. The third evil man discarded the milk-churn covers. The fourth evil man knocked Dumuzid's special cup from its hook. The fifth evil man broke his shepherd's crook. The sixth evil man kicked the milk-churns on their sides and spilt the milk. The seventh evil man smashed all Dumuzid's cups to bits on the ground.

Dumuzid was dead. His sheepfold was deserted.

This was the story of Dumuzid's dream. Dumizid was the shepherd-god and husband of Inana.

Praise be to Dumuzid.
Praise be to the goddess Gestinana, his sister.
Priase be to the goddess Inana.

Mesopotamian mythology was written in both Sumerian and Akkadian, so deities and cities had both a Sumerian name and an Akkadian name. In the table opposite, the Sumerian name is given first, followed by the Akkadian name. The same deities were worshipped throughout Mesopotamia, but some had one particular city where they were believed to live in the main temple of their cult. A variety of mythic traditions co-existed and evolved over 3,000 years of successive Mesopotamian civilisations. The table is not a comprehensive guide to Mesopotamian deities and cities, but it will help readers become familiar with those featured in the stories in this book.

DEITIES AND CITIES

DEITIES		CITIES
Inana Ishtar	*Goddess of passion, action, love, sex, war, violence, power and prosperity*	Unug Uruk
Enki Ea	*God of fresh water and wisdom, crafty god, friend of humanity*	Eridug Eridu
Enlil Ellil	*The almighty god, leader of the gods, 'terrifying force that subdues the land of Sumer'*	Nibru Nippur
An Anu	*Sky-god, source of authority, distant supreme god who lives in the uppermost of the heavens*	Unug Uruk
Utu Shamash	*Sun-god, justice, his 'net spreads over the earth'*	
Nanna-Suen	*Moon-god*	Urim Ur
Ereshkigal	*Queen of the Underworld*	
Dumuzid Dumuzi	*Shepherd-god, dying and rising god, husband of the goddess Inana/Ishtar*	
Nergal	*God of death, war and plague*	Cutha
Namtar	*God of fate*	
Ninlil	*Consort of Enlil, mother of the moon-god*	Nibru Nippur
Ninmah	*Goddess of the womb*	
Nammu	*Mighty ocean mother of everything*	
	The city that was the home of the wise man who survived the great flood and became immortal	Shuruppag Shuruppak
	The city that was cursed by the gods and disappeared completely	Agade Akkad

ACADEMIC SOURCES

The stories retold in this book can be found in academic translations into English of texts originally written on clay tablets in Sumerian and Akkadian using cuneiform script.

SUMERIAN

The Electronic Text Corpus of Sumerian Literature
www-etcsl.orient.ox.ac.uk

Thorkild Jacobsen, *The Harps That Once... Sumerian Poetry in Translation*, Yale University Press, 1987

Jeremy Black, Graham Cunningham, Eleanor Robson and Gabor Zolyomi, *The Literature of Ancient Sumer*, Oxford University Press, 2004

AKKADIAN

Stephanie Dalley, *Myths from Mesopotamia*, Oxford University Press, 1991

Benjamin R. Foster, *Before the Muses: an Anthology of Akkadian Literature*, CDL Press, 1996

Andrew George, *The Epic of Gilgamesh*, Allen Lane, The Penguin Press, 1999

THE ENHEDUANNA SOCIETY

The Enheduanna Society is an education charity established in 2002 to popularise the literature of ancient Iraq through the art of oral storytelling.

Patrons

Dr Harriet Crawford
Dr Graham Cunningham
Dr Stephanie Dalley
Dr Irving Finkel
Dr Lamia al-Gailani Werr
Professor Andrew George
Dr Alasdair Livingstone
Professor Ingrid Lunt
Dr Mohamed Makiya
Professor Roger Matthews
Dr Betty De Shong Meador
Dr Karen Radner
Professor Farouk al-Rawi
Dr Frances Reynolds
Dr Eleanor Robson
Michael Rosen
Rafiq Sabeer
Jenny Uglow
James Ware
Marina Warner
Michael Wood

Trustees

Mohamad Tawfiq Ali
Fran Hazelton
Dilip Jesudasen
Nineb Lamassu
Jane Steedman

P.O. Box 36855
Bloomsbury
London WC1N 1WB
ESoc@zipang.org.uk
www.zipang.org.uk
Registered Charity No. 1097515

SPONSORS

Publication of this book was funded by
the Arts Council England, the Unity Theatre Trust
and the Charlotte Bonham-Carter Trust